The Art Of Christmas

A novel by

Matt Anderson

Also from Matt Anderson

Matt Chat

Matt Chat, Volume 2

Weekend With God

Matt Chat, Volume 3

This book is a work of fiction. Names, characters, places, and incidents either are products of the author's imagination or are used fictitiously. Any resemblance to actual events or locales or persons, living or dead, is entirely coincidental.

Cover Design by Nick Poole

ISBN-13: 978-1490376219
ISBN-10: 1490376216

Acknowledgments

Without reservation, I would have to say that this is the most difficult project I have ever attempted. This is my first foray into fiction, and from the moment of its initial conception to its production took the better part of three years. I pray it's worth your time and investment.

As a reader myself, I rarely sift through this part of the book, as I am anxious to dive into the plot. Reading this is akin to watching a commentary on a DVD from the guy who provided catering service, but I would be remiss to not include some dear people who made this a reality.

Lorene Bowles has been my faithful proofreader for the last ten years. Her expertise of the language is exceeded by her devotion to Christ and passion to help writers. Nick Poole has blessed me with an incredible cover design. He is a gifted designer and pastor. I am grateful for the creative and critical eyes of Katie LeMasters and Carissa Wright who gave me necessary feedback. Scott Murrish, the book you gave helped me in ways you can't imagine. Justin Stentz, your idea was the breakthrough I needed! I also could not have completed this project without the generosity of Jason Leetch.

Finally, I want to thank my family and friends who constantly cheer me on. You know who you are. That's not a throwaway sentence. I try to tell you that as often as I can and will in the future. You are God's tangible gifts to me. Only the Father could make life better than you. Thanks for reading.

One

The evening had all the trappings of greatness. The young couple had enjoyed a delicious Italian meal in a quiet corner of the upscale restaurant, boasting beautiful views of downtown Cleveland and Lake Erie. The view was breathtaking; the atmosphere was inviting; the food was intoxicating. Only one more thing could make this night complete.

Having finished their entrées and splitting a tiramisu, Shelly extended her hands toward the source of her affection for the last ten months. Sheepishly, he returned the favor.

"This was a wonderful meal," she said. "Thanks for going to all this trouble."

"It's no trouble."

She began to stroke his hands with her thumbs, looking into his face while Tyler turned his attention out the window.

"So what would you like to eat on Christmas at my house? My mom says she wants to cook your favorite, no matter what it is. Anything from glazed ham to burgers and fries."

Tyler stared at the tablecloth. "Uh, it doesn't matter. I pretty much like everything."

"Well, if you could give me a little direction, I know my parents will be thankful."

Tyler looked about the room. Everywhere but into Shelly's face.

"What's with you, tonight?"

"Nothing. Just a little too much pasta is all. Makes me want to hibernate." Tyler chuckled at his own observation.

Realizing the moment was romantically spoiled, Shelly subtly released his hands and returned them to her side of the table.

It was a scene that had played out many times over the course of their relationship. At the start, Shelly Franz was drawn to Tyler's artistic flair, intelligence, and witty sense of humor. What she did not realize was that she would make no further emotional progression in ten months.

She decided to try again. "So, I wanted to tell you something." Tyler looked up from the candle he had been eyeing in the middle of the table for the last minute. She made sure she made eye contact with him before she continued. "I wanted you to know that I care for you deeply. I'm so glad we get to celebrate this Christmas together."

Averting her gaze yet again, all Tyler could muster was, "Yeah. Me too."

Shelly couldn't hide her frustration. "Again with this?"

"With what?"

"Nothing, Tyler. It's pointless to bring it up since you don't even realize it's happening."

Tyler leaned in to prevent neighboring tables from gleaning additional information. "What am I doing?"

"It's what you're not doing that bothers me," Shelly said, now leaning forward herself.

"OK, what am I not doing?"

"You're not revealing anything. Every time I start to talk about emotional things, you get physically uncomfortable and barely talk."

"Well, maybe I have a lot on my mind."

"So get it off your mind by talking to me about it. What am I here for?"

"I didn't want to ruin tonight with that stuff."

"Tyler, it doesn't ruin my night to talk to you. If we can't be real with each other, then what do we have?"

Seemingly distracted, he replied, "Huh? Oh, yeah, I guess you're right."

Shelly wiped her mouth with her napkin, placed it on the table, rose from her seat and said, "I'll be back in a few." She pushed her chair under the table with greater force than usual as a means of punctuating her anger.

Though Shelly's diagnosis was correct, Tyler's aversion to intimacy was heightened by his goal for the evening: offering his Christmas present to her. Specifically, a small diamond necklace. It was the first time he had bought her jewelry, and Tyler considered it a big deal. He didn't know how she would receive it. He wanted everything to be perfect. Unfortunately, what he failed to realize was that it already wasn't.

Nervously, he tugged at his buttoned collar. No wonder he hated wearing ties. He didn't know when or how to give it. He was just hoping it would make sense. He debated whether or not to pull out her chair upon her return, but then the jewelry box would be exposed too soon. He decided chivalry could wait. Tyler made one more cursory examination of himself, sat commandingly in his chair (avoiding his usual slouch), and waited for her return.

Tyler Ramsey had spent most of his life on the outside looking in. At least, that is how he perceived it.

Having had more than his share of strife, he had eventually believed life to be a party to which he had not been invited. He seemed to be more of an observer of the human condition than a participant in it. Even when he was indoors, watching life go by through the floor-to-ceiling windows of his fifth-floor loft, he still felt like an outsider.

In his most reflective moments, he pondered just how he had become the man he was. Rolling back through the years in his mind, it was hard to find an era of his life in which he was part of a social herd. Packs never did a thing for him; he was an individualist. The problem was not him, he surmised, but the sycophantic sheep who spent their lives attempting to gain the approval of those incapable of granting it. He had no interest in being one of them.

In elementary school, while most of his peers were involved in a spirited game of kickball at recess, Tyler was busy gathering various rocks from the school property and arranging them into some kind of rudimentary mosaic on the sidewalk. Invitations to "join the fun" were usually met with a raised hand of acknowledgment, no words, and no eye contact. Classmates quickly got the message and left "that strange kid" alone.

Of course, being different also makes one a perfect target. The insults began when he was in the fourth grade; and although he eventually did find a few friends with whom he could find refuge, they could not be with him the entire school day. The danger zones were the playground, cafeteria, and of course, the gymnasium. Tyler often wondered how much easier school could have been without Physical Education. He even sometimes pondered whether there was some type of collusion between gym teachers and psychologists, with the former serving as a funnel to the latter and reciprocal kickbacks from shrinks for referrals. He could not prove the conspiracy, but he surely would have loved to try at some point during his undergraduate studies.

His frequent battles throughout his education had given him a tough emotional exterior; that, and his early family life. He and his mother were a family of two; and even though they were very close and had special moments together, he sometimes kept quiet, still an outsider, still part of a different world. By his best estimation, he had become skeptical at 9, cynical at 16, and downright jaded by the time he finished college. He was quick to believe no one and often congratulated himself for it. It may have seemed to others that he was often depressed, but he wasn't. His world just had a different focus giving him a more reflective frame of mind.

One event seemed to salvage what little sentimentality he had within him: Christmas. In actuality, it was more of a metamorphosis. Tyler would turn a switch somewhere in his mind every late November. His countenance would change; his outlook was elevated. Nothing could take the smile off his face. He loved every part of the season. To him, there was no such thing as a bad Christmas song. Shopping was a joyful adventure, not a chore. Even wrapping presents brought out the artist in him, which was good because he was one.

He had inherited his love of Christmas from his mother. She was the queen of the season. Not only would their home be inundated with multiple Christmas trees and hundreds of lights, but she would also wear festive garb every day and have classic holiday music playing throughout the house. It was a few weeks out of each year that transported their home. Like most single-parent families, finances were less than abundant. It was hard for Beth to make ends meet and pay the bills. And like most single-parent kids, Tyler had grown up way too fast and knew way too much for a kid his age. But Christmas changed that every year! With the tree and decorations, it was as if they were putting a fresh coat of paint over the smudges and scratches of their existence.

Not surprisingly, the largest tree was the centerpiece of the Ramsey house. Beth inspected every tree branch, light, and ornament with obsessive carefulness. She was determined for her tree to be almost magazine-worthy. *Good Housekeeping* was not coming to take pictures, but it was a joy for Tyler to watch her create her masterpiece each year. It must be where his own artistry came from. His mother had long abandoned drawing and painting; but that tree each year seemed to be her cherished canvas, and Tyler thought her the Picasso of the Pretend Pine.

Tyler was fortunate to live in his current space. Wally Bennett, an insurance agent who was a member of the church Tyler sporadically attended, owned the building. His wife Jackie took a liking to the young man's artwork and begged her husband to provide him with an economical place where he could create. Though the building was zoned for commercial use, Wally allowed the aspiring painter to occupy much of the fifth floor for half of what he would pay for a downtown apartment. For the last two years, he had made it his own, finding area rugs, vintage furniture and lamps at yard sales to adorn the former office space. His personal studio was nearest the large windows in the corner. Watching life happen usually inspired him to put paint to canvas.

He had embarked upon this season of life immediately after receiving his bachelor's degree in education. His choice of major was rooted in the reality that few artists can pay their bills. And though his degree would take him to the scene of many early personal wounds, he liked the thought of inspiring kids like himself. Despite the pleadings of his mother who urged him to find a job quickly so as to alleviate her worries for her only child, Tyler decided to take a risk. He wanted to paint more than anything else in the world. Nothing brought him greater joy. To him, teaching was Plan B. It was there for him if his dreams went asunder. Now, he wondered if he was finally at the breaking point.

After 24 months of struggle, peppered by momentary flourishes of creative energy, he had managed to sell only four paintings, three of them to friends or church members who wanted to give him a professional boost. His craftsmanship was nothing less than stellar; but it is simply a hard way to make a living. Financial conditions were tough everywhere so only a few families could afford something as discretionary as a painting. To supplement his income, he turned to waiting tables at a downtown steakhouse. For about 30 hours a week, he would don black pants and a black button-up shirt to relay dinner and drink specials to the upwardly mobile. He did not mind the work, but it took a toll on his creative side. He would go for weeks at a time without so much as touching a brush.

Tyler would often replay the events and decisions of the last two years, wondering if he should have done anything differently. His obsessive nature often caused him to overanalyze. He hated himself for these moments, but they seemed to be his predatory auto-pilot when things weren't going well. To him, it was easier to blame something than nothing, even if that something was him. It was too easy to blame "the economy" or "the market." There must be something he could do to change his fortune.

He had met Shelly Franz ten months ago through a mutual friend who had set them up on a blind date. Though initially reticent in their first encounter, Tyler eventually thawed and displayed his trademark wit which immediately took her in. She was a fan of his art and even posed for a portrait for her birthday present. It didn't seem to matter that he was a struggling artist, unable to purchase the finer things for her at this point in his life. She was just glad to be with him.

Though he was amazed that a woman of such beauty would be attracted to him, he never seemed to be able to find the words or ways to express it. Though she was always forthcoming, Shelly would probe into Tyler's history and was always met with resistance. He had an adept way of using humor as misdirection to evade her questions. When that did not work, he would take the direct approach and tell her he was not ready to share the most intimate details of his life with anyone. She knew there was no point in pushing further. Even if she did, opposition could only follow. Gradually her curiosity of him was giving way to frustration.

As Tyler awaited Shelly's return to the table, he hoped the half-carat diamond necklace would convey what he had not. He had never made a purchase like this before and was assured by the jeweler that it was a great choice for this stage of their relationship. He hoped all the double-shifts and holidays he worked would be worth it to see her face when she opened the box. Feeling the pressure of the moment, he wiped the sweat from his hands with the white-cloth napkin draped over his thigh and placed it on the table.

Shelly returned to their small table and averted his gaze as she sat down. Before Tyler could begin his presentation, Shelly said, "Listen, Tyler, I need to speak to you about something."

Not wanting the moment to be spoiled, Tyler whispered, "Is it really important? 'Cause I have something I want to say, too."

"Yes it is, unfortunately."

Unfortunately? What was this about? Tyler maintained a steady hand upon the box as Shelly asserted herself. It was becoming evident that Tyler was not the only one getting the nerve to say something at this dinner.

"Look, I think we should bring our relationship to an end."

The color drained from Tyler's face. This had quickly deteriorated from a cherished memory to a blindside attack. He could not even respond.

"Something just seems to be wrong in our relationship."

"Wrong? What do you mean? I thought we were fine."

"We really aren't, Tyler."

Tyler was profoundly perplexed. "I don't get it. We always seem to have great conversations, don't we? And we never fight."

"That's kind of the point."

Now he was thoroughly confused. Was she looking for a guy with a temper who could push her emotional buttons? Did she want a bickering partner, a man to trade barbs with for the rest of her existence? He was not that kind of guy. He didn't want to be that kind of guy.

"Tyler, we have been together for ten months, and I hardly know anything about you. Sure we have pleasant conversations, but that is because you are always in control of them. Every time I try to get beneath the surface and learn more about you, you change the subject. What we have is not real for this stage of our relationship. And I can't spend the next months and years of my life wondering if you're ever going to let me in."

Tyler had not moved. His eyes were almost glazed over. Her words barely registered. After her declaration, it didn't really matter what came next. It was all an echo of the first one that rattled in his mind. All he could manage was an, "Uh-huh."

"It's not that I haven't had a good time with you. You have been a perfect gentleman and have treated me better than any man I have ever known. You've been really good to me. It's just that I can't fight against your defenses anymore. I'm sorry."

The tide of anger was beginning to rise within his heart. *Sorry? Really? Ten months of dates, conversations, and love notes, all to be summarized with an "I'm sorry"?* None of these words would form on his lips, however. That was his usual pattern. Growing up in a home in which nothing painful was ever discussed, he had learned the art of avoiding confrontation. To him, arguing was the entry gate into dissolution and separation, ergo if a couple did not argue they did not break up either. As Shelly continued to make her case, Tyler assumed his usual passive stance. Besides, he knew better than to make a scene. What was he supposed to do, talk her out of it? Would debate change the final result? No. He knew better than to fight against the winds of rejection. When they blow, one can only surrender to them. Tyler now believed he was the main course at this meal, elegantly slaughtered and sliced for consumption…and he still had to pay the $100 bill that came with it.

Tyler offered no defense or pleas to stay. He simply uttered various synonyms of "OK" and "I understand." He just wanted the moment to be over so he could go home. Pretending to drop his napkin to the floor, he placed the jewelry box back in his jacket pocket while picking it up, thus assuring that only he would know of his wasteful purchase. How tempted he was to show it to her anyway, plunging the knife of guilt deep into her psyche, but he resisted the evil urge.

Ever the gentleman, Tyler still expected to drive her home. Mercifully, Shelly said she would take a cab home, avoiding the obvious tension that the commute would bring. He remained with her near the front door of the restaurant until the taxi pulled up. As it did, she surprisingly turned to him and kissed him one more time before saying, "Goodbye" and headed out the door.

When he returned to the loft, he thought about the dreaded velvet box that remained in his suit jacket. He didn't know what to do with it. The jewelry store would not refund his money. He would probably receive a store credit, but what was he going to do with that? Besides, he wanted to avoid having to tell the jeweler his "she dumped me" story. It was two days before Christmas, and he once again felt cast in the role of outsider. Losing his girlfriend drastically changed his Christmas plans. He thought he and Shelly would spend Christmas Eve in his loft, where he would make dinner for her and they would watch one of those movies that airs non-stop for 24 hours on one of the cable networks. Christmas day would be celebrated with Shelly's family in the suburbs. Now he wondered how to fill the time without losing his mind. Maybe he could find a way to work a shift at the restaurant Christmas Eve. However, the 25th was now ominously empty on his calendar.

That wasn't the only thing that was empty.

Two hours later, Tyler had still barely moved. He sat at the far end of his vintage sofa, accented with a blanket from his childhood. Still clad in his winter coat and fine-dining attire with the top button of his shirt undone and tie loosened, he obsessed over the jewelry box and what to do with it. Had he been a dweller of Middle Earth, he would have immediately begun a journey toward the nearest volcanic mountain and its lava-filled crater into which he would gleefully deposit the infamous jewelry. Taking it in hand, he continually opened and shut the box, liking the definitive *SNAP!* when it closed. He used to do that with his mom's jewelry boxes when he was a kid. It drove her crazy. He did the same thing with ashtray lids in cars (when cars used to make those things). Beth would eyeball him in the rear-view mirror and snarl, "Tyler, stop it! You're driving me crazy."

"Huh-uh," the then ten year-old would retort, "You're the one driving." He'd give her a wry smile, recognizing his own cleverness. All Beth could do was roll her eyes and get back to the task at hand.

Tyler missed that simplicity, those cute moments between mother and son. He missed having someone humor him. Immediately his thoughts drifted to different times and places, most specifically to Christmases before. He had not allowed himself to dwell on such things for a while, but he needed sentimentality on a night like this. He began to think back to holidays of yore, of Nat King Cole LPs, fudge, and Christmas trees. Ah, those wondrous Christmas trees! Only his mom could make fake pine look so good. He tried to fill in the gaps in his mind with lights and tinsel, trying to recall every detail of her decorative splendor. He closed his eyes and did his best to revisit those exquisite moments as he helped his mother wrap presents for his extended family. And by "helped," he meant putting his finger on the top of the package so Beth could tie a perfect bow with velvet ribbon. Still, it counted; he was assisting. He could not help reexamining every inch of that bygone living room where so many great memories occurred. The old couch (or "davenport," as mom called it), the large-shaded wooden lamps, the end tables with fake-wood covering, the large picture of Jesus over the TV...

SNAP!

Like a cannon shot, the subconscious closing of the jewelry box had awakened him from his blissful trance. As midnight loomed, and with it the arrival of Christmas Eve, Tyler had two choices: stay in this spot for the next two days feeling extremely sorry for himself (which sounded incredibly attractive), or use this moment to his advantage.

From his perspective on the sofa, he looked to his left to the corner of the room where the windows and studio were. He looked at the dormant tools of his trade and wondered if this was the moment to reawaken the catatonic artist within. Tucking the jewelry box in the pocket of his winter coat, he removed it, his suit jacket, and tie and walked to the barstool by the easel that held a blank piece of canvas. He exhaled loudly as he thought about the daunting task before him. For the last two years, he had decided to paint strictly for commercial purposes. Every color, every stroke was devoted to the purpose of hanging in some patron's living room and having it meet their approval. Now, he would paint for himself.

Wanting to recapture what had only moments before grabbed his imagination, he decided he would try to paint his family's living room at Christmastime, with the decorated tree given the greatest amount of space and detail. It would not be difficult. After all, it had been the centerpiece of his favorite time of year every year. It elicited the best of feelings within him. Perhaps committing this to canvas would lift his spirits as well. Maybe from the ashes of rejection could come something wonderful.

He started painting.

Two

Tyler decided to intentionally make the tree three times larger than the other items. Though the logical part of his brain begged him to reconsider, the young painter quelled his inner critic. "If I want the tree big, I'm gonna make the tree big," he said to himself. That was how he saw the living room as a child. He could focus only on the tree and little else. Rolling up the sleeves of his white oxford shirt, with brush and palette in hand, he closed his eyes and tried to remember the annual scene. Though he was tempted to give the tree a surreal quality, he decided to keep it as accurate as possible, in spite of its distorted size. He needed the real thing right now, and he needed it to be bigger than life.

This was not the kind of painting at which Tyler excelled. He enjoyed having a subject before him to study and duplicate. He could also craft a scene or design completely from his imagination with no original to which it could be compared. He loved the security of the one and the complete abandon of the other, but this presented a challenge. He wanted to replicate his childhood experience, but he was feeling anxious about it. His fear of doing it wrong had to be overcome by the fear of not trying at all. Like a writer with fingers hovered over the keyboard, he knew the first stroke had to be made, good or bad.

He mixed green and black and constructed long vertical lines down the center of the picture to depict the central pole of the tree, complete with holes in which to insert the individual pine pieces. He mulled over how many "growths" emerged from each metallic "branch" and their unique upward slope at the tip to help hold ornaments in place. It was a painstaking process, as he intricately crafted each individual needle. Usually, the artistic process was initially difficult but gave way to great momentum as he progressed. This project was draining the strength from him. He believed it had nothing to do with the late-night hour. Many artists will tell you that the best time to create is in the middle of the night. No, this was something altogether different.

He had to push through every line and brushstroke. His own body and mind seemed to be fighting against him. Every 20 minutes, he would take a break and lean against the window to observe his progress, then discipline himself to go right back to it. He could not fathom why this project was so emotionally draining. By 2 a.m. he was completely exhausted. The mental energy expended in remembering the exquisite detail of the tree and the emotion he was feeling from the devastation earlier that night had taken its toll. The undecorated tree was finished, and he was satisfied with what he had done to that point. He felt as if he had wrestled and subdued some sort of powerful sea creature.

Now he would have to adorn the fake pine with lights, tinsel, and of course the ornaments. The garland would be easily recreated, and he had some lights strung in the loft that came from home. But the ornaments. That would be a bigger struggle to remember. He recalled his mother having a mixture of red, green, blue, gold, and silver balls made of twine – most the worse for wear – as part of the yearly rotation. And there were other ornaments of varying shapes and sizes, most of which he could not place at this hour. The tree had taken so much out of him that he felt fresh out of brain cells. He felt an urgency to finish this painting in one sitting. He thought he might lose the nerve to continue if he paused, but he wanted it to be done accurately as well. It was as if his mother had made a beyond-the-grave appearance and quipped, "Now Tyler, remember! We never do a halfway job!" It was one of her truisms that, had she ever done social networking, would have been on the list of quotations on her "About" page.

Frustration overwhelmed him. Alas, the sea creature seemed to resurface and was exacting revenge upon his vessel and kinfolk. Tyler practically threw himself onto the sofa, leaned his head back against the wall, and exhaled. He had not even begun to process the events of the evening, and he was not about to start now. He had a different way of dealing with his pain. His thoughts were completely absorbed in his new work, and he desperately needed to remember those ornaments if he had even a shot of accomplishment.

Then it hit him. The storage shed. Everything from the old house was there, untouched since its arrival. It would be about a ten-mile drive, but he knew exactly what he needed. The facility had 24-hour access, and his uncle had been kind enough to pay for the unit until Tyler decided what to do with his "inheritance." He didn't feel like going back out again, but his newfound work ethic would not allow him to stop. As he weighed the pros and cons, he had what he would later describe as a moment of clarity. As long as he was going to retrieve the Christmas decorations, why not construct the entire tree in his apartment and have the real thing before him as a subject? On a night filled with unexpected detours, this may have been the strangest. However, the spontaneity of it oddly appealed to him. Putting on his winter coat and grabbing his keys, he headed out the door and to his car in the apartment's downtown parking garage.

Riding through the desolate streets of downtown Cleveland, Tyler almost laughed at himself as he muttered, "Who would have thought that I would be doing this tonight?"

He turned on a local radio station playing all-Christmas music, if for no other reason than to provide necessary noise. Driving south on Ontario, he soon came upon Public Square, the unofficial central hub of Cleveland. Most of the time, the traffic is so intense that one dare not avert his gaze from the car ahead; but tonight afforded a different opportunity. The Square was so beautiful at this time of year, and Tyler rarely had time to appreciate it. Rather than go straight through it on Ontario, he turned right on Rockwell Avenue. On his right was the historic Old Stone Church. On his left were innumerable trees illuminated in red and white. He made a left turn onto West 2nd Street and headed toward the Terminal Tower, Cleveland's most iconic building. Bathed in green and red light much like the Empire State Building in New York, he was overwhelmed by the colors around him. On his left, he could barely make out the statue of city namesake Moses Cleaveland in the darkness. The official Christmas tree seemed more than happy to soak up the attention of the southwest quadrant. Turning left on South Roadway, he headed to the least-decorated southeast corner and the memorial to Civil War soldiers and sailors. Crossing Superior, he looked again to his left and saw the northeast quadrant adorned in bright green and white. It elevated him to a calmer place. Christmas lights always seemed to do that for him. Turning left on Rockway, then left on Ontario once again, he headed toward the Interstate 71 interchange and eventually the suburbs and the awaiting storage space.

Swint Brothers Storage was not far from Hopkins International Airport. It was also only two miles from the Ramsey family home in Brook Park. It provided round-the-clock access to its renters for moments exactly like this. Using a swipe-card to get past the front gate, he pulled his car in front of Unit #326. Each space was actually a single garage door, secured by a padlock. Unlocking it and lifting the orange door, he beheld all the physical vestiges of Elizabeth Ramsey.

For at least a minute, he surveyed the scene, scanning left to right at objects that had peppered his life for its first 18 years. He had not seen it for the past eight months. Only a few of the boxes were labeled, since it was up to Tyler to complete that chore. Packing them was difficult enough, let alone providing a detailed inventory of each container. His preference would have been to do it alone; but when people are grieving, many feel the need to bark out orders at others to give the illusion that they are in control of something. His Aunt Rita and Uncle Adam were the chief offenders. Appointing themselves the acquirers and keepers of the family relics, they hounded him for weeks after the funeral, literally supervising him to decide what was to be donated, sold, thrown away and kept. Of course, there seemed to be a few items that his relatives wanted for themselves, which also seemed to be the point of the entire home curation. Every plate, every washcloth, every toy, and every blouse was accompanied with the usual interrogative, "So what do you want to do with this?" Any hesitation was met with boisterous disapproval. "Come on, Tyler! We have a lot to go through before we can transition the house." After snatching Beth's fine china for themselves, everything else seemed for them to be the equivalent of a Saturday morning flea market. He was in no emotional position to make such huge decisions.

Near his feet in the storage space laid an office supply store box. He noticed it had no labeling. Foraging through it, he took a mental inventory that it included trinkets such as spiritual figurines, placemats, and napkin rings. Though he wished he could have extracted each item to savor a glorious memory of it, those moments had been overlaid by the larger-than-life heads of his officious aunt and uncle that fateful day. As he remembered it, each of them hovered over one of his shoulders and seemed to be shouting in both ears, "Let's go, Tyler! Why does this have to take so long?" He was being treated like a compulsive hoarder who was living up to his chin in old *Redbook* magazines and fast-food wrappers. What Tyler wanted to say was, "Because, unlike the crap at your house, something here might be not only valuable but also precious to me!" Of course, that kind of self-assertion would once again be buried under an avalanche of accommodation and contrition. He would hurriedly choose a fate for each item in a rush to be done with it all and repeatedly apologize for not going faster.

Tyler uttered apologies as often as folks from his mother's generation said "Uh" and his generation used the word "like". It was the most powerful passive weapon in his un-arsenal. He had figured out years ago that a quick apology could prevent or end an argument, which to him was a great moral achievement. At all costs, an end to hostilities must be achieved. It really didn't matter who was in the wrong. For him, it wasn't a question of fault but a matter of peace. Tranquility was king. Whatever cost to him was simply collateral damage to the bigger objective of harmony.

Knowing he had largely failed in the task of labeling his mother's boxes of belongings, he knew this might be a greater challenge than he first believed. Fortunately, his quarry would not be so difficult to find. His mother was a much better organizer than he. The tree itself was in a rectangular box, the same box provided by the manufacturer. All the other accoutrements of the Ramsey holiday display were in a series of four green rubber bins. As if that was not enough of a giveaway, Beth had taken the opportunity to write "CHRISTMAS" in black marker on each of them. Tyler smiled broadly as he remembered her efficiency.

Stepping around the stacked contents of the room like a solider tiptoeing through a minefield, he managed to avoid damaging anything around him and stacked the green bins outside the garage door. Bringing out the tree last and lowering and padlocking the door, Tyler stuffed his ten year-old Dodge sedan with his Yuletide booty – two bins in the trunk, tree and bin in the back seat, and one bin in the front passenger seat.

He prayed a curious policeman wouldn't pull him over on his way home. That would be one odd explanation.

Returning home, he parked his car and kept the elevator open so that he could load all the boxes in one trip. He was an expert at such feats, having navigated many a grocery day toting 12 bags of items in one fell swoop. He had to admit he took personal delight in such achievements. From the elevator, he carried the tree box then each bin individually into his apartment. He lined them up in front of the sofa. Removing his coat, he sat down and opened the Christmas tree box, hoping to make some three-dimensional art this night.

The assembly directions for the tree had long been lost. He extracted the tree's base and quickly found the central pole and inserted it. That is where any sense of ease would end. As in his painting, the pole had holes into which the individual pieces would be inserted. At one time, the pole was littered with colors that matched the painted metal ends of the pine pieces. However, much like the printed instructions, the colored paint on the pole and pieces had long faded away. Like everything else this evening, Tyler would have to do this the hard way.

He removed every branch from the box and individually straightened each offshoot to make it look as authentic as possible. This was the painstaking work at which his mother excelled, while he grew increasingly impatient. But he knew he had to push through. Nothing this evening would be left undone. Once straightened, the pieces of the tree were laid out on the wooden-looking tile floor from longest to shortest, thereby providing him the best chance to align the tree correctly. He began to insert branches into the pole. This had been his mother's exclusive domain, so he soon realized that this was his first solo effort.

Once it was completely assembled, he manipulated the pieces and shoots to fill in the tree as thoroughly as possible. It didn't take long for him to realize that this would be far beneath his mother's standards. Truth be known, Tyler thought most of his efforts were far beneath his mother's standards. She was a loving and nurturing mother, but she demanded a lot from Tyler in all phases of his life. Maybe it was his being the only child and, by default, the bearer of all his mother's hopes and dreams. Maybe it was her insistence on his not being like the father he barely knew. Having been on his own for a few years, he was better able to see those demands in a different light, but growing up under those pressures was no day at the beach.

Clearly, even this artist did not have the know-how to make this piece of fake foliage more fashionable. He felt the same frustration when he made peanut butter and jelly sandwiches for himself. Nothing he did or tried to do could compare to how his mother did it. She just seemed to have that magic touch on everything she did. Tyler wished he knew the feeling.

Realizing it was the best effort he could possibly make, he sat back down on the couch and compared his construction with the painting he had made earlier. His painting from memory was grander and richer than what he had physically accomplished in his apartment. An odd monument for an odd night. Another wave of self-pity crashed against the shore of his mind. He could not resist feeling the pangs of rejection from the hours and now years before.

"This is quite a life I lead," he said. He surveyed the landscape of his living space and inner life and began to draw dangerous conclusions. "Let's see if I got this right. I'm a twenty-four year old unsuccessful artist living in an old office space with no girlfriend, no prospects, and no money." He grabbed his winter coat off the sofa, reached within the pocket, and pulled out the dreaded velvet box. "And now my newest addition to the collection: A diamond necklace I can't even give away."

He returned the box to its odd new home in the front pocket of his coat, laid it on the other side of the sofa, leaned his head back, and brushed back the formation of tears. He had not cried since the week of his mother's death months before. This was the closest he had come since. It was a painful but necessary moment in Tyler's journey. He just did not realize it yet.

Three

Sometime after ten in the morning on Christmas Eve, Tyler was awakened by the "rat-a-tat" sound of someone lightly drumming their fingers against his heavy front door. Tyler instantly knew who it was. Righting himself, he slowly stepped to the entrance, released the deadbolt, turned the knob and opened the door to his surprise guest.

It was Wally Bennett, his landlord and benefactor. Wally was about 5 inches shorter than Tyler and on the portly side. His salt-and-pepper hair, complete with mustache and beard gave him an air that only added to his dignity. Persistently optimistic, he was rarely seen without a smile and his trademark guttural laugh that most people found intoxicating. His insurance agency office was on the ground floor of this building, a building and business that passed from previous generations.

Standing proudly in the entryway, Wally sported his usual short-sleeved, buttoned dress shirt with a decades-old tie that, at its longest, would still be a far cry from his navel. That never seemed to bother Wally, however. He would never be mistaken for a model. Besides, the short thick tie and his bigger-than-life enthusiasm seemed to give potential clients a feeling of competence and safety. This is a no-nonsense, salt-of-the-earth guy who cares more about my well-being than his wardrobe, they would assume. He had this folksy way about him that transcended business. Instead of in his office talking about deductibles and payment options, one felt like they were on the front porch with an old friend, drinking a glass of iced tea. No wonder Wally was so successful. What Tyler could not deduce was whether Wally knew the method behind the madness or he just backed his way into prosperity.

Wally was not tactful in his assessment of his tenant's haggard appearance. "Wow! You look pretty ragged."

Tyler sauntered back to the sofa and collapsed onto the middle cushion. "Thanks, Wally. You always know the right thing to say."

"Sorry, buddy." Wally couldn't help but chuckle to himself, and as he did his belly couldn't help but bounce in equal delight. "My wife always says I need to give my brain a chance to catch up to my tongue." His familiar guffaw filled the apartment.

Tyler was not in a laughing mood. He rubbed his eyes with his hand, then used the same hand to run through his matted hair a few times before focusing on his uninvited guest. "So what's up?"

As Wally surveyed the loft, he looked at the remains of what had been a long night. A bare Christmas tree, boxes and bins intermittently scattered about the floor, his studio light on over his easel. Tyler still donned most of the suit he had sported the previous evening, sans jacket and tie. But from the rumpled nature of his presentation, Wally was not sure whether Tyler was wearing the suit or it was wearing him. "I am guessing that last night was either the best or worst night of your life, but I have no idea which."

"Take a wild guess," Tyler quipped. He tended to be a bit punchy without adequate sleep.

"She didn't like it?"

"No, I never even got the chance to show her the necklace. She dumped me last night." Tyler leaned forward, placed his elbows on his knees and covered his face with his hands.

"Oh, Tyler." One thing Wally was good at was empathy. It was a rare gift, and Wally had it in spades. He set Tyler's winter coat on the carpet and sat next to his tenant on the sofa. He put an arm around his shoulder. "I am so sorry."

Tyler kept his hands to his face, more out of fatigue than sorrow. Wally was not sure what to say next, so he said nothing. Again, a rare and wise choice. He knew anything that came out of his mouth at this moment would only make himself feel better, not the devastated young man next to him.

They remained there for about ten minutes. Wally wondered whether tears would flow, but none were forthcoming. Eventually, Tyler inhaled deeply and began to sit back. Wally removed his arm and remained where he was. Anxious to break the tension, Wally asked, "So what now?" It was an intentionally vague question. Tyler could take that in one of many directions. What would he do now about a girlfriend? What would he do now about the necklace? In what direction would his life go now? He decided to let the young artist paint in the empty spots.

"Now I call the steakhouse and tell them I can work tonight."

This was not the direction Wally thought he would go. "Tyler, you shouldn't work tonight."

Tyler thought about that for a few moments, then looked over at the skeletal tree that had seemed to mock him the night before. "That's true. Besides, I have a Christmas tree I have to finish."

Wally couldn't let the moment pass without inquiring. "Yeah, and speaking of that..."

"Oh, yeah. One of my adventures last night."

"Well, I guess it's better than a lot of other things you could have done."

"I suppose. I probably wouldn't have done any of those right either."

Wally did not know what that statement meant and decided not to pursue it. "So you're going to decorate that old Christmas tree?"

"Yeah. One way or another." Tyler slid a couple of bins toward him, opened the lids, and began to sift through the contents within. Wally watched in fascination. Tyler pulled out old ornament boxes with the aforementioned balls of twine. They had definitely seen better days. Tyler removed the cover and pulled out individual ones to inspect. Many of them had been snagged and lost twine in one fashion or another. Some had large clumps of it dangling from its host. Some were only half-covered with styrofoam clearly visible underneath. With each box, Tyler would only shake his head in mystery.

"You know," Wally said in an effort to bring levity, "my mother always liked to say that every ornament has a story."

"And apparently, the story of these ornaments is, 'Attention, discount shoppers: defective ornaments on sale for the next 10 minutes.'" Wally put his lips together, unsure if there was a good way to communicate with Tyler at all right now. "I don't know why mom held on to these."

"I'm sure she had a reason. Are there any more?'

"Yeah, I'm sure of it. We had a variety of things. She would offset the colored-thread items with handmade ornaments." Tyler continued removing Santas of varying sizes, Norman Rockwell holiday coasters, unending strings of lights, and the nativity scene that was always placed on top of the television in the living room of their home.

"Tyler, I don't want to short-circuit your plans, but I have decided that you are not going to spend the next two days on your own. I won't hear of it." Every so often, Wally would shift into paternal mode, and Tyler had no choice but to receive it with grace. "When I close up shop this afternoon, I am taking you with me back to the house for a get together I am having with some friends from church. Then we'll head out to our congregation's Christmas Eve service."

This definitely was not the holiday Tyler had planned. His mind whirled in multiple directions, trying to think of some way to extricate himself from what promised to be a difficult evening. Nothing against the church or the Bennetts and their ilk. He just was not in the mood to be even remotely charming. He feared his cloudy presence could subdue the holiday spirit of all in a ten-mile radius.

"And before you can say 'no,' if you go with us tonight, I'll forego your rent for January." Ah, the ultimate trump card for a starving artist. It was the first hint of hope Tyler had received.

"I just don't want to be a drag on everyone tonight is all."

"You won't be. Just try to wear something else, OK?"

Tyler couldn't help chuckling a little. Wally, thinking he had struck comedy gold, released a belly laugh that might have been heard in his office four floors below. Tyler smiled and said, "OK, Mr. Bennett. What time should I be ready?"

"We leave promptly at 3. I'll come by and pick you up."

"OK, see you then," Tyler said as they both headed toward the door. Wally, never one to belabor the moment, opened the door and headed toward the elevator. Tyler closed the door behind him, turned around and leaned against it, looking over his loft and the scene of chaos it had become. Unsure of what to do first, he walked over to the corner windows to see how fellow Clevelanders were spending their Christmas Eve. Being near one of the few remaining retail areas of the downtown area, he watched from above as last-minute shoppers carried loaded shopping bags as they moved from store to store. "They look like they're accomplishing something," Tyler surmised. He wondered what it would be like to be them, walking somewhere with confidence. He muttered, "People with shopping bags are definitely happier than those without shopping bags. They know people, have lists, make conversational party favors, know how to whip up great eggnog, and have their kids' names professionally sewn into Christmas stockings. They go to a mall, knowing they won't come away empty-handed. They even walk with greater purpose." Tyler wished he was a shopping bag kind of guy. However, what little disposable income he had was reflected in a velvet box he seemed doomed to keep. *Little to buy with and no one to buy for.* That thought was so depressing that he immediately turned from the window and became determined to accomplish something. He had a few hours before Wally came back. So he peeled away the remainder of the suit that he had worn for the last 18 hours, put on a T-shirt and sweat pants, and came back to the Christmas bins.

It took the excavation of three bins, but Tyler finally found the other ornaments he knew existed but could not exactly recall. One by one, he would remove an ornament from the bin, sit back, and carefully examine it. None of them could have been mistaken for pieces of art. Though in better shape than the balls of twine, the value of these trinkets was solely sentimental. The problem was that they were not sentimental to him. Apparently the Christmas tree he had envisioned and remembered on canvas was a bit ambitious. Maybe the memory of the tree wasn't his after all. Perhaps he had idealized his childhood existence to such an extent that he willfully ignored the nicks and scrapes now obvious to him.

His painting had been more impressionistic than he realized. And now the authenticity of it all was just one more crushing blow he did not need. In comparison to the emotions of the previous night, however, this was but a ripple. He knew those times were special, and nothing could change those memories. He refused to allow the harsh reality to change what had been precious to him; much like his relatives' berating had done shortly after his mother's death. But would there be more disappointment to follow? Dare he venture into this unknown terrain? What spirituality he could muster to this point in his life was now on full display. He felt guided by something higher than himself. Perhaps this entire scenario was diagrammed by God Himself. Maybe this was a grand quest that only he could complete. Maybe there was a deified agenda here. Maybe he was akin to one of the great adventurers of literature or film. Is it possible that he was being selected, plucked from obscurity for a higher purpose? Would this be the moment that he was confronted with one of life's great principles? Would there finally be resolution in his unending composition of dissonance?

As usual, however, his sporadic optimism gave way and he emotionally crashed to earth. "Yeah, right!" he said aloud. "You're not Luke Skywalker. You're a messed-up kid from Cleveland who's trying to put together a stupid Christmas tree, for heaven's sakes." Though his journey was suddenly much less lofty, he decided to continue, delusions of grandeur notwithstanding.

Returning to the ornaments, he resumed his careful inspection, placing less emphasis now on why they were retained and more on remembering when and why they had been attained.

There was a crocheted Santa head, handcrafted by his grandmother. Not that her skill was all that proficient, but the hobby gave her great delight. At least once a year, Tyler could count on at least one crocheted item to find its way into his decor or even wardrobe. If it wasn't a winter hat, it was a striped afghan for his bed. But those blankets did little to bring him comfort on cold, winter nights. Grandma's knots were so loose that the "covering" was fraught with large gaps wide enough for cold air to penetrate during the night. When his mother wasn't watching, he'd sneak a larger comforter from the linen closet and place it between him and the afghan. Inevitably his plan would always fail, however. His constant motion in bed during the night would eventually cause the lighter afghan to slide off and onto the floor at his side. His mother would see the evidence each morning. He was never in trouble, of course. Beth just wondered how to explain it if and when the afghan's creator should be the one to discover the crime scene one day. Tyler chuckled to himself as he thought about those mornings and the vain attempts to proudly utilize his grandmother's props.

Maybe Wally was right. Maybe there were stories to these dilapidated decorations, but the narrative behind them had long been lost. In fact, he could vaguely remember when his mother had bought or had been given the ornaments. As he looked at his cell phone, he roused himself and realized he had spent the better part of twenty minutes dwelling upon memories evoked by a crocheted Santa head. Tyler had to be careful lest he risk being transfixed for hours and not ready for his ride to the suburbs.

He went against the current of his artistic mind and decided to prioritize. In the time left, he would bear down and finish decorating the tree. He wanted to be able to come home to a finished product. Then he could finish his painting and sleep in heavenly peace, or some derivative of the famous carol. Remembering the natural order of things in the Ramsey household, the lights would go on the tree before anything else. His enthusiasm would be quickly tempered as he would pull out all the strings of lights tethered together in a giant ball of cords. He didn't know if it was Christmas lights or a likeness of his lower intestines. To assist in the untangling process, Tyler played some Christmas music from his computer. "Whatever helps," he muttered to himself.

It must have helped because no less than 20 minutes later, the innards had been properly extracted. Before stringing them on the fake pine branches, he remembered the trick his mother utilized and plugged them all in first. He kept them plugged in while decorating. Although it would not provide the big Tada! moment that people love with Christmas trees where with a pull of a switch the entire thing is suddenly illuminated, it also prevented the disappointment of having the finished product then realizing that one of the bulbs is out of place thereby rendering the entire string useless. Tyler didn't need a "Voilà!" He just wanted to get it right the first time.

Once the lights were finished, Tyler put on the silver tinsel that had seemed to predate his birth. It had clearly been smashed and crushed in any number of ways from dozens of packings and unpackings. Tyler decided to allow it to be a symbol of his own life – crushed, imperfect, but still worthy of the big room.

He was on a roll now, buoyed by his progress. All that was left were the ornaments. Knowing he couldn't take the time he had with the Santa head, he alternated between balls of twine and the random ornaments of varying sizes and styles. He tried his best to intersperse them throughout the tree.

"And Tyler, don't forget to do the back the same way you do the front," he could hear his mother saying.

"Aw mom," he'd complain every year, especially when he was very young. "Who's gonna know?"

"Santa will know," Beth would quip, and that always ended the argument. How can a kid argue with wanting to impress Santa? After all, he would eventually see the place. He didn't want a shabby back-half of a Christmas tree to nudge him over to the Naughty List at the last possible moment.

As he would delicately place each ornament in its rightful spot, he could only take the time to glance at them. He was more concerned with whether its attached string would be thick enough to embrace the circumference of the branch.

There was the big pine cone ornament that was always awkward to fit among the others. There were the two tin silver bells that were a staple of the Ramsey Tree. There was a house fashioned from popsicle sticks. He knew he made that one at some point. Finally, he pulled out an ornament shaped like a Bible. His mother had an incredible fondness for it and what it represented. As memory served, only Beth would put this one on the tree each year. It was deeply personal to her. She put it near the top and always made a statement like, "Tyler, we have to hold the Word of God high in our lives." He would nod approvingly, unsure of what it meant. This was no short-lived pronouncement. Beth made a habit of reading and studying the Bible. On Sunday morning, her favorite TV preachers could be heard as she was getting ready for church. Those guys with layers of hair-spray and Southern accents really fired her up. As they would stride to the car to head to church, her black-leather King James was at her side like a Colt pistol strapped to a Dodge City sheriff. Following her instructions, he put the Bible ornament as high as it could go. And just like that, he was done.

He took a few steps back to take in the view. This was the proudest Tyler had been of himself in some time. He knew it wasn't nearly as good as his mother's efforts, but it wasn't bad for a rookie either. He decided to be pleased with it and sat on the sofa for a while to admire it. After about 20 minutes of beholding his faux-botanical masterpiece, he glanced to his studio where a partially-finished painting awaited him later. Knowing Wally would be dropping by within 10 minutes, he stacked the bins on the lesser used end of the loft and managed to bring some sense of order for the first time in a few days. It was a cathartic experience for him. It seemed to improve his mood, to realize he was so close to his goal.

Little did he realize how much was left to be done.

Four

His mother and his church taught him one thing; life taught him something else. Probably the best way to describe Tyler's relationship with spirituality was on-again, off-again. For most of his childhood, he remembered having to go somewhere on Sunday morning.

Initially, his family attended the Congregational Church. The pastor, Reverend Matznick, had served as the spiritual shepherd there for more than 25 years. He wore an oversized robe with huge sleeves that gathered at his elbow when he was gesturing exuberantly, then collapsed back into position when he grabbed the edges of the lectern to look over his notes again. Though he would never be mistaken for a revivalist preacher, Matznick earnestly believed in what he was saying. He had a certain charm that Tyler, even in his early years, could discern.

First Congregational had weekly communion, but Beth would restrict Tyler from participating. The young boy was almost mesmerized by the big golden plates being passed toward him with the small glasses of juice (or, at least he thought it was juice) and the smaller tray of bread (or, at least he thought it was bread). Almost every week when the ushers came forward to begin distribution, Tyler would turn to his mother and, in his most hopeful expression, ask, "Can I, Mom?" Each week, she would close her eyes and shake her head in disapproval. Most weeks, Tyler would relent, hoping to wear her down as the weeks and months elapsed. But every so often, he would follow up her refusal with a, "Why not?" His mother would lean down close to her son's ear and whisper, "Because you don't understand the body and the blood." That one always got him. Other than sounding like a bad name for a horror movie, he had no inkling as to what she was saying. He decided that this part of the service wasn't for him, until somehow he was able to magically divine what "the body and the blood" meant, because his mother didn't seem to want to tell him.

Tyler made his first spiritual choices when he was eight. While he was still in elementary school, his mom had signed him up for a Vacation Bible School that the local Baptist church was sponsoring. Tyler was too compliant to say it aloud, but how could anyone put "vacation" and "school" in the same sentence? It was the ultimate contradiction. The two concepts were naturally at war with one another. So the "Bible" part must have been thrown in to balance the two. Who's going to complain about "vacation school" when the Bible is in the middle of it? Tyler recognized a few kids from school, but most he was meeting for the first time. He did not see himself being there to win friends. He was on a mission.

On Monday, the first day of the VBS, it was announced that there would be a contest for each age group of kids at the event. He would be in the division for seven and eight year-olds. The concept was simple: The kid with the most points wins. These types of competitions brought out a different side of Tyler. Normally sanguine, the idea of winning something – anything – would raise his antennae and fire up his internal engine. Points would be awarded for attendance, bringing friends, reciting the daily memory verse, bringing your Bible, and giving in the offering. Tyler knew this was his kind of competition. When sports were involved, the uncoordinated shy boy would plead to forfeit. But when athletics were removed from the equation, it was his perfect chance for revenge against those who had humiliated him in kickball, dodgeball, basketball, or any "ball" for that matter.

He was completely focused the entire week. He listened intently to the Bible stories, just in case there were surprise questions for points. He memorized every assigned verse, though they got progressively harder each day. The first day's, "Love your enemies" gave way to, "All things work together for good to those who love God," in the middle of the week and finally John 3:16, the Bible's most famous verse, on Friday.

It was during the teaching related to John 3:16 that something unexpected happened. The teacher explained that Jesus loved us all very much. So much that he decided to die for us so we wouldn't have to go to hell. That might have been all Tyler heard that afternoon, because his mind began racing. He was thinking about all of his church experiences to that point in his life. This certainly was not the first time he had heard anything about Jesus. It was just the first time it really meant something to him. After the lesson, the teacher was talking with Tyler about his experience at VBS when Tyler blurted out, "I want to ask Jesus in my heart." The teacher, a woman who Tyler could only think was at least in her nineties, was unruffled by the outburst. She asked if there were others who were interested in doing the same, and a handful of other children responded. After a prayer from the teacher and one from Tyler, he was in! He even received a tract to take home that simply said, "SAVED!" on the cover. He was so excited to get home and share the news with his mother. It was the most joyous he had ever seen her.

On Friday night, there was a special rally with all the children and parents in attendance to announce the winners and, to the surprise of few, Tyler won his age category. He was awarded with a leather-bound copy of the King James Version of the Bible, and they had even gone to the trouble of engraving his name on the front cover. It was a victorious moment indeed. When they got home, Beth took a pen and, on the inside cover of his new Bible, wrote his name and the date of his conversion. "This is so you never forget," she said, wiping a tear from her cheek. Tyler was not sure why she was so emotional, but he let it go in these kinds of circumstances.

Beth and Tyler stuck it out in the Baptist church for a couple of years after that, but then suddenly Beth announced to her son one day that they would be leaving Peace Baptist and going elsewhere. Tyler was unsure of the reason, and Beth did not provide one. She had rendered a verdict, and there was no veto. She had heard from a co-worker about a charismatic church in town, and since that seemed to be more akin to Beth's personal style, they would be making the move to Grace Cathedral. Its pastor, Dave Duncan, pulled no punches. He was not afraid to take stances on issues, be they political, social, or spiritual. The hundreds in attendance each Sunday were right behind him.

Though he couldn't grasp it at the time, Tyler would later describe it as an odd transition. On the one hand, he was thankful to have a Sunday morning that was more "spiced up" than the Baptists, but he sometimes tired of what he perceived to be a free-for-all in the Pentecostal service. Coming from Peace Baptist where the most demonstrative gesture was a nod, Tyler was initially rattled when he heard people respond verbally. And it went beyond the usual "Amen" or "Praise the Lord!" Some were known to say things like, "Glory!" or "I know that's right," and even the occasional, "Mmmhmm" which Tyler never truly deciphered.

Grace's teachings about the security of the soul were in stark contrast to what he heard even as a youngster at Peace Baptist. His previous church had taught him that no one could remove him from God's hand. Grace Cathedral taught him that we could remove ourselves from His hand. In college, he would tell his friends that his spiritual history had gone from "once saved, always saved" to "if saved, barely saved".

Admittedly, most of the concepts being taught from the pulpit went over his head. However, when Pastor Duncan would get on a roll about certain issues or sins, Tyler was completely focused. Hardly a month went by that his pastor didn't rail against cigarettes and going to theaters. Of course, he would always put the emphasis on the second syllable, so it sounded like, "thee-A-ters". The boy wasn't sure what went on at thee-a-ters, but it must have been bad. He and his mom often went there to watch kids' movies, especially in the summer. Everything seemed to be aboveboard to him. Maybe they were selling cigarettes at the thee-a-ters. A double whammy! Tyler would make a mental note to ask his mom later about this but always forgot.

Tyler's pastor usually seemed a little upset about something while giving his sermons, which was strange because he was such a nice man everywhere else. Though he had no understanding of theology or the deeper concepts of scripture, Tyler derived two conclusions from his weekly visits to Grace Cathedral: God was mad, and Tyler would never measure up. To add to his spiritual anxiety, occasional references in sermons would be made to a giant screen that would show the whole world every wrong thing he had ever done. The boy felt doomed. He never broached the subject of the big screen with Beth, for he feared having to discuss what would be on it. And though a boy of ten could hardly do many things worthy of shame, the young lad often felt it to be a death sentence.

It wasn't all bad at Grace. Eventually, Tyler got involved in the youth group. He was fond of Steve, his youth pastor. Steve, in an effort to maintain informality with the teenagers, insisted on the students not using the pastor title when addressing him. His mom was not fond of the policy, often interjecting that it was the ultimate sign of respect, even if "Pastor Steve" didn't realize it yet. Tyler made great friends and did all the typical youth group activities, including car washes, home Bible studies, performing in a drama group, and even taking a week-long trip to Mexico to help the poor. Steve encouraged his artistic side, telling him he had great potential. Tyler was unaccustomed to receiving compliments from men, so he often didn't respond to such praise and averted eye contact in moments like that. Secretly, he was glad to receive it.

Through his teenage years, it became obvious that Tyler was much more tied in to Grace Cathedral than his mother. He wasn't sure why, and she never offered an explanation. By the time he was 16, it was clear that she was there for his benefit and not her own. She just didn't seem to connect with the faithful there anymore. By the time he could drive and had his own car, Beth would leave right after service, head home and start preparing lunch, knowing Tyler would get home about an hour later. She wasn't the most open person in the world, but neither was Tyler. The only difference is that Tyler knew how to maneuver through a room of people whereas his mother rarely tried. She was often misunderstood, and Tyler was left being her Public Relations agent with the rest of the congregation.

Sometimes Tyler couldn't fake it either, especially when others in the church offered their unsolicited opinions about him and his mother. He never understood where people mustered that kind of gall. Only in that setting could random acquaintances have the courage to say such harmful things. This happened with greater frequency after Beth was diagnosed. A couple of "saints" cornered him on one occasion, opining that his mother was now suffering because of her divorce years before. Maybe it was the shock from the chutzpah of such a comment or the place in which it was said, but Tyler would sheepishly look down at the floor and take the verbal assault without rebuttal. When the salvo ended, he would swallow hard and walk away.

One Sunday would change him forever. After service, he was talking with some of his friends in the sanctuary. They were talking about getting together at a mutual friend's house when a church leader interrupted their plans. "Uh, excuse me. Tyler?" Tyler looked at the fiftyish woman with respect. She was a Sunday School teacher and a fixture at Grace for decades. "Yes, ma'am?" he replied. With a wave of her hand, she beckoned the high school senior away from the herd. They were about thirty feet away from any listening ear.

"Tyler, I've been doing a lot of praying about your mother," she announced. Tyler was immediately on edge. He balled his hands into fists inside his pockets. He tensed up, like he was about to sustain a blow. "I want you to pass something on to her, because I never seem to get the chance to tell her directly," she continued. "I know it's been a struggle these last few months with her illness, and I know we as a church have prayed for her repeatedly; but it has only been in the last week during my private Bible study that something became clear. Tyler, God's Word tells us that without faith it is impossible to please God. When I read that verse a few days ago, all I could think about was your mom."

Tyler had no idea where this was going.

"I believe the reason your mother is sick is because of a lack of faith."

The young man could only stare in complete disbelief.

"I have been so frustrated," she pontificated, "that our prayers don't seem to be working. We have tried everything we know – fasting, anointing her with oil, having her on the church's Prayer Chain for some time now, and there's no healing. It became clear to me that the problem isn't with us; it's with her. The only thing preventing your mother's healing is her faith. Her lack of faith has displeased the Lord and so she remains sick. I know that's difficult to hear, Tyler, but I want her to be healed as much as you do. Please pass this on to her, OK?"

Obediently, Tyler nodded and the woman walked away. No wonder his mother made a dash for the car every Sunday. How many conversations like this had she endured and never repeated? A switch flipped at that moment and, without addressing his friends, he walked out of the sanctuary, through the lobby, straight to his car and never looked back. As he drove home, he unleashed his rage, not so much at the spiritual busybody who had proclaimed judgment upon his mother's spirituality, but at himself for standing there and taking it. That seemed to define his whole life: standing there and taking it. Taking it like a man - a weak, powerless, ineffective little man.

It took a while for him to regain his composure and go inside his home where Sunday lunch was waiting. There was no way he was going to repeat those nefarious words to his sick mother. A few days later, he made a pronouncement he had crafted that awful Sunday, but purposely waited to say it aloud so that his mom wouldn't be suspicious. "Mom, I hope this is OK, but I don't think I should go to Grace anymore."

Beth almost dropped the plate she was washing back in the sink. "Why? What's wrong? What happened?"

"Nothing. It's just that I'm 18 now and feel ready to make some big decisions for my life."

"Honey, I know you're an adult and have a good head on your shoulders, but this is a pretty big decision. Are you abandoning church altogether?"

"No, not at all, Mom. I just think I'm done at Grace is all. Don't worry. I'll find a new place to go. Besides, it frees you up to go to Calvary Fellowship. You've been talking up that place for a while."

"Well, maybe you can go with me there, Tyler."

"Yeah. Maybe." Truth is, Tyler was not going to go anywhere. Though he didn't necessarily hold God or even Grace Cathedral responsible, he never wanted to be put in that position again. He never wanted to hear from superficial saints who apparently spoke on God's behalf. In quieter moments, he wondered if what the awful woman said was true. Maybe God was displeased with them. Maybe there was too much stuff in his life already doomed to be on the big screen. God had to be displeased. There was just no other conclusion he could make. He didn't know how to summon the faith required to get on

God's good side again. Though he wouldn't walk away from what he believed, what he now believed would keep him from darkening the door of a church whenever possible.

The church tried their best to woo them back. The obligatory "We miss you" letters and the phone calls from church leaders were peppered with pleas from friends within the church. Without being specific, Tyler only replied, "We've just chosen to move on." Eventually, they gave in to his demands. Tyler circled the emotional wagons and privately vowed to never attend church again.

That rule was broken after his mother's death. He felt a sense of obligation on her behalf to give church another try. He went to First Community Church downtown and, try as he might to avoid all personal contact, the Bennetts served as greeters and made it their personal mission to involve themselves in his life. For Tyler, they had been a rare lifeline in a sea of judgment.

And now, the full weight of Tyler's agreement with Wally was dawning upon him. It was all coming back this Christmas Eve night. As he cleaned and dressed, he now fully realized what he was subjecting himself to. Though Wally and his wife Jackie could not be painted with the same prejudicial brushstroke, he had no idea how many uncouth, untactful churchgoers he would have to speak to throughout the course of the evening. While he would sit prone on someone's living room couch like a wounded antelope in the Serengeti, vicious predators could come at him from all directions, all of them speculating on his mother's death and her lack of faith that caused it. Maybe some spiritual giant would surmise that it was he who brought about her death, his departure from church ultimately sealing her fate. He was not ready for such exchanges. He was not ready to have his life summed up in pithy statements and Biblical slogans. In the interest of saving a few hundred bucks, he was going to subject himself to a breed of people he deemed the unhealthiest on earth. In short, it wasn't Christ who bothered him – it was Christians.

Tyler channeled his fear of interaction into presenting himself in the best manner possible. If he was completely insecure on the inside, he could at least sport a patina of self-assurance. Having been to a number of Sunday services there but not a Christmas Eve, he wasn't sure what the unofficial rules were going to be, so he fell back on one of his personal rules of presentation: better overdressed than underdressed. Sporting a black button-down shirt, black slacks, and a gray, three-button jacket, he had to admit as he looked at himself in the mirror that he had come a long way from the rumpled refugee he saw only an hour before. At least he would have the appearance of someone who had his life together.

Rather than wait for Wally's prompt knock on the door, he surprised his landlord by descending to the Ground Floor and the offices of Bennett Insurance. His secretary had been given the day off, and Wally was filing some last-minute claims as Tyler strode through the inner office door.

"Well, young man," Wally admitted, "You are looking pretty sharp, I must say. I'd better stay close to my wife tonight so she isn't tempted to leave me for a younger man." He let loose with his usual exhaled burst of laughter, and Tyler smiled in response to his unbridled zeal. When Tyler needed insurance (not to mention assurance), he knew whom he would call.

"You're too much, Mr. B." Tyler said, looking down at the floor, as was his habit when confronted with affirmation.

"I mean it!" Wally put on his overcoat, grabbed his keys and briefcase, and backed Tyler out the door. "Aren't you going to wear your winter coat?"

"Nah, I should be all right."

"Oh, to be young and warm-blooded," Wally said, amused with himself. "Let's head out."

As they walked to Wally's assigned parking spot on the first level of the parking garage, Tyler asked, "So, what's the agenda for the evening?"

"Well, first we'll head over to the homestead. I'll try to put the finishing touches to the house while you help my wife with whatever she needs in the kitchen."

"Oh, so that's why you brought me along," Tyler jokingly inserted.

Another belly laugh from Wally was followed with, "You're on to me, kid! No, I just figured you would want something to do besides stare at the TV screen."

Actually, the whole TV thing sounded pretty good to Tyler. It would afford him with the perfect opportunity to look completely preoccupied, thus eliminating chances for idiotic interactions. They arrived at Wally's six-year-old blue sedan. Like Wally, it was frugal and understated. No client would ever think he was making a mint off their backs.

"Our home group friends will be over at around 4:30. We'll have dinner together at the house then head over to the church for their 7:00 Christmas Eve service. After that, who knows?"

Eating at 4:30. This must be what it's like to hang around the nearly retired. "Sounds great," Tyler said, not knowing how his digestive system would handle heavy food at such a foreign time. Good thing he was hungry.

Silence ensued for the better part of the trip to the Bennett home in Fairview Park, partly because Wally was tired from the day and partly because Tyler was terrible at interacting with older men. It had plagued him from childhood. Being with his mother had taught him how to communicate with women, but those rules seemed to be forgotten when he was with a man his senior.

Wally finally broke the stalemate. "You OK with all this, Tyler?"

"With…?"

"With spending the better part of an evening with a group of people you don't know?"

"Yeah, I think so. Have I met all these people at church?"

"I'm not sure, Tyler. You rarely stick around to let me introduce you."

"Yeah, I know. Sorry I'm not very chatty."

"It's all right by me. Just glad to have you there." Sometimes Wally Bennett's approval was so easy to attain that it almost seemed unreal. Tyler smiled as he turned his head toward the passenger window to look at the landscape of West Cleveland.

Wally pulled into the driveway of his unsurprisingly modest home. It was no palace but had been maintained well. Wally and Jackie had lived here from their earliest days of marriage. Though they had no children, they loved each other and threw themselves into their church community. Their mortgage was paid off, and they were focused on planning for retirement. They were the poster-children of the American Dream. This man must have been who Norman Rockwell had in mind when he created his illustrations.

Knowing company would be arriving, Wally pulled forward to the back, unattached garage, leaving as much room as he could for his guests. Tyler, always on the lookout for escape routes, thought if he had driven here, he would have parked on the street for a quick getaway, in case things got dicey. However, there would be no hasty exits tonight. As they walked through the back door, the young artist could easily spot Jackie Bennett holding court. She was Tyler's biggest and, to his knowledge, only fan. Her fiery red, aerosol-sprayed hair and fair complexion were an easy giveaway to her Irish roots. Born Mary Alana O'Fallon, her father, an ardent supporter of John F.

Kennedy, took to calling her Jackie when she was a baby after the First Lady. Demure by nature, she was always the perfect leveling force to Wally's exuberance. While her words were consistently understated, her clothes were not. Jackie always knew how to make a splash with her wardrobe choices. Even the slightest special occasion would bring out something in sequins. She fascinated Tyler. In every other way, she resisted attention, but her fashion would not be denied. And Christmas Eve was no exception. Tyler anticipated a *tour de force* of kitsch on this occasion, and Jackie did not disappoint. Her green turtleneck was overlapped by a bright red three-dimensional sweater depicting the famous reindeer Rudolph. How did he know it was Rudolph? From the nose that protruded out of the sweater and blinked with a red light inside. This would be a new benchmark for her. Tyler was thankful they weren't going out to eat. The sweater might set off sprinkler systems. The capper was the seasonal green apron that bore an inscription in red that proclaimed, "Yule love this grub!" Sometimes Tyler wasn't sure how complimentary it was that she liked his artwork, but he often reasoned that you don't argue over benefactors. In spite of her odd fashion sense, she was a very sweet woman. Though never realized, she had a natural maternal instinct that just waited for the right audience. Tyler had been that recipient many times, especially over the last year. She and Wally had hosted the starving artist at their home after church for lunch on a few occasions. Each time, Tyler was visibly uncomfortable when he arrived but completely at ease by the time he left.

She was supervising a number of pots simultaneously cooking on the stove, each of varying sizes and degrees of steam emanation. As they crossed the threshold, Wally couldn't help having a little fun at Tyler's expense. "Hi, good lookin'! I hope it's OK, but I picked up this homeless guy downtown. Normally I wouldn't, but he was so well-dressed I figured he couldn't be too much trouble."

This was the routine: Wally ribbed and Jackie rescued. "Now Tyler," Jackie offered as she strode toward the young man, untying the gaudy apron to reveal the garish aforementioned sweater, "You don't have to take that from him, you know." She gave him her usual peck on the cheek, as she did with all visitors to her home.

"I know, Mrs. Bennett," Tyler said, looking at the floor in deference for the humbling welcome he received.

"And please! Enough with this 'Mrs. Bennett' stuff. It's Jackie."

"Yes, Mis-, I mean, Jackie."

"That's better." Jackie had returned to her laboratory, complete with ostentatious labcoat. "Wally, let's not leave our guest in the entryway. And you need to get ready, by the way. Everyone will be here within the hour."

"I am ready."

Jackie exhaled in frustration and looked at Tyler for assistance. "Do you see what I have to deal with on a daily basis?"

"What?" Wally replied, now also looking at Tyler for help. Tyler could only shrug his shoulders in an effort to be Switzerland in this debate.

"You're not wearing that suit you've worn all day to the Christmas Eve service. I have your red sweater and black trousers sitting on the bed. Shower up!"

Not wanting to prolong hostility, innocent as it was, Wally headed past his wife and to the interior of the home. On his way he couldn't help noticing Jackie's highly-touted divinity fudge sitting on a baking sheet on the countertop next to the stove. Not wanting to wait for the guests to arrive, Wally began to extend his hand toward the sweet concoction when he felt the swift blow of a wooden spoon on the top of his hand. Drawing his hand back with nothing to show for his efforts,

Wally could only offer, "All right; I'm going," and slunk back to the master bedroom.

Fully appreciating the moment, Jackie turned her head to Tyler and said, "That's how the nuns used to do it to us in parochial school," widening her grin and returning to her task.

By now, Tyler had found a place to sit at the dinette table, where the hosts enjoyed most of their meals in their glorious simplicity. Tyler envied them. How wonderful to have life figured out, to be done striving, clawing, and scratching to find your niche in this world. To be done with debt and doubt and be in a place where wisdom and experience are highly valued by others. It must be a wonderful place. Life made more sense when he was here; not so much on the 5th floor of an old office building.

"Tyler, hang up your jacket and go find a comfortable spot in the living room. Don't stay here on my account."

Tyler went to put his jacket on the coat rack by the back door, but he had to put it on top of one of the others already hanging, since every peg was already taken. He returned to his seat at the dinette and asked, "Miss-, uh, Jackie? Sorry. I keep forgetting."

"It's OK, sweetie. What can I do ya for?" This was one of Jackie's trademark lines when she sensed someone needed her help.

"How do you know when your life is going the right direction…or the wrong one, for that matter?" As was his pattern, it was easier for Tyler to ask such things of the woman of the house than the man.

Jackie, recognizing an important moment when she heard one, immediately changed all the stove settings to simmer and sat next to her guest at the dinette table. "What's wrong, sweetie?"

This was hard for Tyler. He rarely let anyone through the veil in his life. It's why he still had an unclaimed necklace in his apartment. He never knew whom to trust, so he usually chose no one. But if there was anyone he could bring in from the outside it was this couple. Still, the events of the previous day lingered, and he thought about the confusion that awaited his return home. He wanted to bolt from the scene, immediately regretting posing the question. "It's nothing really."

"Nothing?" Jackie took his hand. "I know better than to believe that."

In retreat, Tyler tried to dismiss the moment. "Nah, you should get back to your responsibilities. It can wait." This was an all-purpose escape clause that usually worked. Tyler had discovered early on that people were mostly fixated on themselves and their tasks and, if he ever wanted to get out of a jam, he would appeal to that absorption.

"Tyler, when someone implies that their life is out of sorts, you don't abandon them to check on a marinade." Jackie could never be accused of circling the airport conversationally. Tyler appreciated her candor.

"It's just that when I look at you and Mr. B, I see something very different from what I'm living every day."

"Well, of course! You're just starting out. Wally and I have been around the block a few times. It comes with the territory."

"But it's more than that," Tyler responded. Then he paused for a number of seconds, constructing his words carefully. He made sure to look down at the beige tablecloth as he began to share from his heart, worried that maintaining eye contact with Jackie might unnerve him. "It's just that I can't remember a time when I've really lived life, you know? To me, life isn't something you do; it's something that happens to you. I hear people talk about life being full of choices, but I haven't had any choices."

Tyler's voice crescendoed with each sentence. "Choices have been made for me, whether I liked it or not. People make decisions on my behalf, and I'm supposed to like them, while God sits in silence, apparently agreeing with the whole arrangement. I read silly slogans like, 'Life is an adventure' and think that my life reads more like a pamphlet. I'm not an adventurer; I'm a patient strapped to a dental chair, waiting for God to use his next sharp implement to probe, scrape, and inflict pain!"

The young man had become so boisterous that Wally, wearing a T-shirt and jeans with remnants of shaving cream on his face and a towel around his neck, quickly returned to the kitchen. He didn't say anything but remained framed in the doorway watching the proceedings, wanting to see if his beloved needed his help. It was a rare outburst from a young man who seemed always in control of his faculties. Out of sorts, Tyler briefly looked up and saw the middle-aged couple expectantly staring at him, unsure of what to do next. Knowing he had created an uncomfortable moment, he offered, "It just always seems like life is happening to me without my permission."

Jackie glanced at her husband and patted the tabletop twice, a non-verbal cue for him to join her at the table. "Tyler, Wally told me about last night, and I am so sorry. You deserve better than that. I won't even try to make you feel better with some of those ridiculous things we Christians say sometimes. It hurts, and that's all there is to it."

"But it's more than that," Tyler said. "It's everything. It's all the family stuff, the divorce stuff, the sickness stuff…" Tyler's voice trailed off as he unintentionally removed an emotional scab. "I just feel like such a pawn."

Wiping his face clean with the towel around his neck and setting it aside on the table, Wally addressed their guest. "Tyler, I don't want to try to say we know what you're going through, because our lives have been very different from yours." Taking his wife's hand and holding it on top of the table, he continued. "But I remember some dark times over the years, right, Ma?" Jackie nodded and ceded to her husband, who knew how to rise to the occasion.

"A long time ago, during our first few years of marriage, we went through a time of numerous miscarriages."

Tyler suddenly looked up, his eyes glued to this effervescent man whose tone had shifted into something more sobering than he had heard from him to that point.

"It was a terrible time. Either we couldn't conceive or something would happen early on to end the pregnancy. We were devastated. Even took it out on each other, too." Wally looked at his wife to make sure he had his facts straight, and Jackie agreed as her eyes welled up with tears. "We felt cursed by God. I remember searching through the previous years to figure out what I had done to displease Him so. I wanted to fix whatever sin I had committed. I hardly spoke to my wife or to God. Being in church was painful, and I just went through the motions."

"On top of that," Jackie added, "there were a few people in our church who didn't help the situation." She sighed as she revisited painful quiet corners in her heart. "I had one person who felt bound to tell me that I was having miscarriages because I was slightly overweight back then." Now Tyler was locked in. "Do you believe that? I wanted to give her the business end of a family Bible, if you catch my drift." It was amazing to watch this couple. Normally, Wally was the jokester and Jackie the pragmatist. But in these kinds of situations, Wally was incredibly stoical and Jackie was the bringer of levity.

Tyler chuckled then quickly stopped himself for fear of appearing insensitive. "I can't imagine someone being that callous. You must have been tempted to leave the church."

"Yeah, for a few days we were; but then we realized that if we try to avoid stupid people the rest of our lives that we'll be changing churches every month." This time Jackie howled at her own observation.

Wally patted her arm to bring her back to the reality of the moment. "It took a lot of time to get healing from that, especially when we realized we were never going to have children. And I posed lots of questions to God that He didn't answer. He does that, you know?" Tyler closed his eyes and nodded in affirmation. "I finally came to a point of realizing that some things happen because there's evil in this world, some things are allowed because they cause us to depend on Him more, and others happen because of decisions other people make. Sometimes the last group grieves God more than anything else; and while He won't take away our free will (because doing that would make Him a liar), I think He takes those situations and finds ways to weave us back to where we belong."

"I'm just not sure my life is that easily explained," Tyler reasoned.

"There's nothing easy about it," Jackie inserted. "Faith is never easy. Believing seemingly takes no effort, yet so many don't make it. That's because it's all effort. It's betting your life's philosophy on the improvable. It's the simplest and most complex thing in the universe. Without it, we have nothing. With it, anything is possible. Tyler, maybe God is going to use these events to get you back to where you need to be. Maybe He wants you to really believe again."

This inspired Wally. "That's right. Maybe God is going to do whatever it takes to convince you that you matter to Him."

"Well, He's certainly going about it the wrong way."

"I can assure you," Jackie added, "when He starts doing it, you'll know it."

Not much more could be said after that. Both Bennetts simultaneously rose from their chairs. Wally patted the young man on the back and returned to the bedroom to change. Jackie kissed him on the forehead and said, "I'm so glad you're here tonight." A few seconds later, she continued. "Well, we'd better get crackin'. Everyone will be here soon. Tyler, could you help me set the table?"

Tyler dutifully assisted Jackie in putting the final touches to the place settings and beverages. Within a half hour, the guests had arrived and dinner was served. Since the Bennetts occupied each end of their rarely-used dining room table, Tyler resolved to be next to one of them. For this meal, it would be Wally who would serve as his life preserver. He managed to handle the dinner conversation well, occasionally answering questions about his artwork and future plans. Of course, Jackie was more than happy to be his press agent, urging their friends to stop by his loft and purchase one of his paintings.

As dinner moved into dessert, Jackie announced, "All right, everyone. I have a number of desserts prepared for us, but it is self-serve. Feel free to take some, as well as a glass of punch and find a place in the living room." The guests obeyed and, within five minutes, were seated around the living room with dessert plates on laps and punch cups in hand. It was then that Jackie continued her unplanned junket of Tyler's work. "Pay special attention to Tyler's painting above the mantle. You'll note that it's a pastoral scene." This was followed by the requisite oohs and ahs of the guests that Tyler dismissed as forced courtesy to the host. "Someone look closely at the bottom of the painting, and you'll notice one of Tyler's trademarks. He very subtly titles his works there, blending it into the scenery. He actually paints the title first on the canvas. Isn't that wonderful? You have to look closely." One of the guests volunteered and, standing only a foot in front of the painting, scanned its base and said, "Here it is! 'Peace Field'. Is that it?" Jackie delightfully congratulated her correct answer as the others joined in applause.

Not wanting to be in a position of receiving forced praise, Tyler took a piece of Jackie's divinity fudge and returned to the dinette table he occupied before the guests arrived. He always got fidgety when people starting asking elementary questions or tried to analyze him through what was on the canvas. He'd sit this one out and hope someone would become a future customer.

Tyler put the small, red plastic plate on the table, took a drink of the cherry punch and stretched out his arms, pacing himself for what lay ahead. Taking the divinity from his plate, he privately wondered how long it had been since he had eaten this dessert. He reasoned that it had been years. Biting into the semi-hardened exterior, it quickly gave way to a softer, flavorful middle with strong hints of vanilla and almond nuts. Suddenly, taste buds that had been dormant now came alive within his mouth, reminding him of why he had always loved this Christmas treat. Tyler couldn't remember the last time something tasted so refreshing.

Only then did he remember.

Five

As far back as Tyler could recall, financial problems had been a constant tether to his existence. From the moment his family went from three members to two, Beth had a mantra that was repeated thousands of times over the course of Tyler's childhood: "We can't afford that!" Tyler remembered hearing his mother speak with friends at home or on the phone about her financial situation. From those conversations, the young boy could eventually assess their financial health, depending on the phrase she used. In descending order, they went from "paycheck to paycheck" to "down to our last nickel" to the bottom rung, "flat broke."

As is common in homes of divorce the custodial parent, often lacking adequate adult social contact, confides too much in one or more of the children. In those transparent moments, Beth would occasionally update her son on their financial challenges. She would speak freely about not being able to pay creditors or fret about utility bills. She would rant about owed alimony and back child support, but Tyler had no grasp of either concept. Beth had no idea how those conversations would echo in her son's mind when he would try to go to sleep. He would obsess over such details. Though too young to know the ins and outs of fiscal maneuvering, he would ponder the potential consequences for hours at a time without the knowledge or skill to alleviate the fear.

His worry would expand due to conversations his mom had with others. Often Beth would be on the phone complaining about other people's children and how they had no appreciation for the things they had or would go through clothes and shoes too quickly. Tyler, ever internalizing, decided he would not be one of those kids. He would never ask for anything of the sort. Frequently Beth would have to discover Tyler's belongings in a state of disrepair to alert her attention to his needs. On one occasion, as Tyler was walking through the house, it was obvious that the sole of his left shoe had separated, creating almost a sandal-like effect.

"Tyler, what's wrong with your shoe?"

"Huh? Oh, nothing."

"Nothing? You can hardly get around in those things."

"I'm fine, mom."

"No you're not. Why didn't you tell me your shoes were in such bad shape?"

Tyler realized the answer to that question was more probing than his mother could handle. All he knew was that he didn't want to be one of "those kids." He did not want to be one more difficulty in his mother's life.

In spite of her occasional lapses of sharing inappropriate information, Tyler knew there was a lot that was kept from him. Beth often had a lot on her mind; the weight of the world seemed to be on her shoulders. Hardly a day went by when money wasn't part of the family discourse. Early in life Tyler learned to associate nickels and dimes with headache and heartache.

Already seen as an outcast by his schoolmates, Tyler's lack of resources showed in his wardrobe choices (or the lack thereof). Some of his middle school peers took to calling him "Rerun," since he had a much smaller rotation of clothes than most of the other kids and often wore the same few outfits. Even sitting with his small circle of friends in the cafeteria, he made it a practice to eat his lunch quickly. He didn't want any of them to investigate the contents of his sandwich and realize that the only items between the two slices of bread were condiments.

That was the extent of the social damage done to him from the Ramseys' abject poverty. Tyler reasoned it could have been worse. What limited the devastation was the fact that Tyler had stopped trying to climb the ladder of popularity at school, thus lowering his visibility. His lack of wealth didn't hurt his reputation, but rather cemented it. For him, school was a place to exist and survive. Achievement was negotiable, but the ship of social acceptance had sailed long ago.

There were occasional moments, however, when Beth crossed the line. A combination of a lack of income and poor money management often left his mother at the breaking point. She had bounced more than her share of checks around town and had been outlawed by a number of stores from writing any more. This would not necessarily deter Beth, however.

"Tyler, get your shoes on. We're going to buy groceries."

"Aw, Mom. Do I really have to go?"

"Yes. Hurry up. We don't have all day."

Tyler was surprised by her insistence. She usually liked to shop alone. That's because Tyler had a penchant for constantly begging for anything with sugar and/or chocolate. Beth figured it was easier to leave him at home than to play "bad cop" at the store all the time. Though only ten years old, Tyler had mellowed significantly from his toddler tantrums. Maybe this was his mother's stamp of approval on his behavior.

Nothing seemed out of the ordinary the entire time they walked through the aisles, accumulating food, household items, and toiletries. Just before they made their way to the checkout lanes, however, his mother pulled out her checkbook. She began writing all the information needed, except the amount. As she did, Tyler couldn't help overhearing her utter, "I sure hope they take this." At ten, Tyler had little idea what that meant, not to mention the intricacies of personal banking.

Beth became very quiet as she loaded their items onto the conveyor belt where the cashier would scan each one and send it to the bagger. Tyler knew something was amiss and wanted to impress his mom by not even asking for a pack of gum from the "impulse buy" rack. As the total was announced, she began filling in the amount portions of the check. Avoiding eye contact, she tore it out and handed it to the cashier. Reading the check and the name associated with it, the cashier began consulting a pre-printed list taped to her station. Tyler couldn't quite make them out, but it appeared to be a list of names. Beth continued to look down at Tyler, intentionally averting the cashier's gaze. Tyler could only look back and forth between the two ladies, unsure of what was transpiring. The cashier, still holding the check in her right hand, suddenly turned from the list toward his mother, opened her mouth to speak, but then quickly closed it. The cashier looked down at Tyler's beaming face, and a smile slowly crept across her own. She processed the check, handed Beth the receipt, and said, "Have a good day."

Beth speedily wheeled the cart to the parking lot as if she had completed a bank heist. She wanted to load the groceries in the trunk and drive off before the cashier changed her mind. It was only after Beth's death that Tyler realized he had been used as a prop on that occasion. Though admittedly for a good cause, being used by another cannot be completely excused; and the incident still left a faint sting after all these years.

Admittedly, Beth had few professional options. Armed with only a high school diploma, it was difficult to find work that could support an entire household. Her pressures would have been lessened had her ex-husband James been more faithful in fulfilling his court-mandated obligations. However, the electric company could care less about the ex-husband's check being late. She explored a number of options. One was at the local steel plant, working in the office on the 3-11 shift. Beth's mother would watch Tyler; once he fell asleep, she would go home. The hope was that Beth would get home by 11:30

p.m., and Tyler would be none the wiser. Her perfect plan quickly fell apart as, more than once a week, she would pull into the driveway to find her son kneeling backwards on the living room couch with his face against their large front window, sobbing for her return. The paycheck was not worth the guilt and inconvenience. She quit after a month. There would have to be another way.

That opportunity came a few months later with a local company called *Bellasario, Inc.*, which was a smaller outfit that fashioned plumbing supplies. Beth would work as a bookkeeper in their main office in West Cleveland. It was a 9-5 shift, which meant that Tyler would have to be alone only a couple of hours after school. Television cartoons would have to fill the brief parental gap until she walked through the back door from a hard day's work. Her son quickly adjusted to the new routine and was relieved that most of his mother's financial worries had been alleviated.

Of course, it still meant saying "no" to almost any of the extras offered to Tyler. Whether it was school or church-related, the young man had to miss out on a lot. He never complained about it; but then again, he never really complained about anything. Not being the athletic, outdoorsy type, Tyler wasted few tears on missing youth camp. He was able to go on a missions trip but only because he had raised all the funds necessary. When it came to other trips or events or concerts, however, it was difficult for him to hear his peers speak in glowing terms about what he missed. It was further evidence that he would forever be the little kid with his forehead against the glass watching life go by and wondering what happened to the people he loved as he sat at the window crying.

Tyler was eleven and Thanksgiving was approaching when Beth had a difficult announcement to make. As they ate spaghetti and garlic bread one evening, Beth said, "Well, it looks like Bellasario is laying me off." Tyler had no idea what that meant, but he knew it was bad by observing his mother's fallen countenance. "Orders have been down, and with the new year approaching they have to make some cutbacks."

"You mean you're losing your job?" Tyler asked.

Beth could only look down at her plate. "Yeah, that's what it means."

Ever the source of comfort, the boy said, "I'm so sorry, Mom. I know you liked working there."

"Well, it's more than that, sweetie. It means we need God to come through again."

That line mystified Tyler as much as the one with "laying me off." He had learned that when his mother said something with "God" in it the best thing for him to do was just nod, even if he didn't understand the content. To make the mistake of asking her a follow-up question meant a guaranteed twenty-minute dissertation on the latest book she had been reading from one of the TV preachers she so dearly loved.

"This is just God's way of getting our attention," Beth proclaimed.

Really? By making us homeless? Tyler wondered why the Almighty would play such ruthless games as that. To keep peace, his private doubts were rarely aired in Beth's presence.

She continued her spiritual stream-of-consciousness reasoning. "Yes, siree. He definitely has our attention now. And when He has our attention, anything is possible. We just need to pray, Tyler. We just need to ask God for what we want and for His will to be done."

Tyler was completely befuddled. Ask God? Tyler could not even ask his mother for a pair of shoes. How was he supposed to kneel down somewhere and ask the Creator for a job for his mother…or anything, for that matter? Besides, the Lord of All had some explaining to do of His own. After all, He was the one who stood by while Tyler's family fell apart. It was He who failed to act day after day while Tyler was being socially exiled and ridiculed at school. It was He who sat on His hands when his mother had to choose between buying food and keeping the gas from being shut off. Though he loved his mother more than anyone in the world, whatever she was selling right now, he wasn't buying.

His internal tirade was interrupted when he felt the touch of his mother's hand on his arm, forcing him to lower the forkful of spun spaghetti that had hovered above his plate for over a minute. Beth leaned forward toward her son and had his full attention. "Sweetheart, I want you to listen to me. I don't know how long it's going to take to find another job. I don't even know if I'll find another job. If things get bad enough, we might have to leave this place." That was understandably unsettling to the young man next to her who was growing up way too fast. "But there's a difference between a house and a home. A house is only a structure." She gestured around the room at the walls and ceiling. "This," as she pointed to Tyler and herself, "is a home. Nobody can take away what we have here. So I don't want you to worry about anything, because no matter what…" Beth's eyes began to fill with tears and her voice was noticeably impacted with emotion. "No matter what, we will always have a home." She grasped his arm again and smiled as a tear escaped her right eye.

Tyler loved it when she spoke this way. It was the most protected he would feel in his childhood. Later he wondered whether his mother was trying to convince him or herself. Either way, he appreciated her determination. A few days later, in his art class, his instructor reminded the youngsters that Thanksgiving break was soon approaching.

"Now, I don't know when all of your families decorate for Christmas, but chances are, most of you won't do so until the Thanksgiving holiday at the earliest. With that in mind, I want to challenge you to create a Christmas ornament that you can take home to your parents and put on your family Christmas tree this year."

Tyler thought this was a great idea. He knew how much his mother treasured ornaments, and he had instant inspiration for his creation. His teacher had put out a vast array of art supplies on a side table. Studying its contents, Tyler chose a few tools with which to fashion his masterpiece. He would keep it simple, opting only for popsicle sticks, glue, two colors of paint, and a brush. The budding artist wished art class could last long just like football players hoped for all-day gym class. Once he was locked in, he could shut out the rest of the world, focusing only on his workspace and asking for no assistance from a classmate or teacher. He even had a habit of hunching over the table so that his face seemed only inches from its surface. He knew it give him the air of being a mad scientist, but he was too focused on the task before him to pay it any mind.

After the final bell that day, Tyler went to his locker, retrieved his book bag, and rode the bus home. Though he knew his mother wouldn't be there waiting for him, the anticipation of her arrival was just too exciting. The two hours of waiting felt more like two days. Seconds after Beth entered the house, dropping her purse on the floor next to the back door and hanging her coat, she was confronted by a smiling eleven-year-old. Beth surmised that this could mean one of two things: Either Tyler had done something very wrong and was trying to warm up to her quickly, or her son was genuinely excited about something. Both occurred so rarely that it would take Beth a few minutes to decipher which it was.

"I want to put up the tree tonight," Tyler announced.

Immediately Beth's face fell. It was a Tuesday night. She was exhausted from her day at work, and the last thing she wanted to do was drag boxes out of the attic and act festively. "Oh, Tyler. I am beat. I'm going to order a pizza because I don't even feel like cooking. There's no way I want to get into all that tonight."

"But Mom, I really want to."

Beth carefully examined her boy's expression. This was the happiest she had seen him in a long time. She was wise enough to know that, however she felt, when your kid is anxious to do something productive, go with it. "All right, but you're gonna help, OK?"

"Of course, Mom. Don't I always help?"

Beth rolled her eyes at his precociousness but quickly set it aside. "Give me a second to change and we'll get into the attic."

"Yes!" Tyler shouted, accentuated with a pump of his fist. Beth had no idea where all this enthusiasm came from, and frankly she didn't care. This was one of those golden moments that rarely fall into a parent's lap after a child turns ten. While Tyler watched, she made up a batch of her divinity fudge and put it in the oven. The pungent vanilla smell would fill the house as it heated in the oven and while they decorated in the living room.

For the next few hours, the team of two lugged large boxes and bins from the attic to the living room. Beth gained a second wind after the pizza was delivered and consumed, regaining her Queen of Christmas posture. Tyler maintained his energy throughout, even changing Christmas CDs as each one ended. He followed all of her orders and even had a few ideas of his own that were gladly welcomed.

When the large tree had been completed and the living room lights were turned off so that the architects were bathed only in hues of red, blue, green, white, and gold, Tyler had a sudden realization. "Wait, Mom. We forgot something."

Beth painstakingly looked up and down the tree to find what had been forgotten. "I don't think so, honey."

"Yeah we did, Mom. We forgot an ornament."

Doing a cursory examination of the room and boxes, Beth could only surmise, "There's no way we forgot one."

Tyler, still with that mischievous grin on his face from hours before, left the room and came back seconds later with a wad of crumpled red tissue paper in his hand. "We forgot this one!" He put the paper in his mother's hand and sat on the couch to see her reaction.

Sitting next to her son, Beth opened the tightly gathered paper and looked inside to see what her son had actually been up to. Inside was an ornament. It was simple but meaningful. Tyler had fashioned a house out of popsicle sticks and glued them to a small wooden backing. He painted the roof green and the outer wall of the house red. It was done with great precision, and Beth was overwhelmed.

"Remember what you said, Mom? We may not always have a house, but we'll always have a home."

Beth held the new treasure to her heart and was visibly overwhelmed. "I think it's absolutely beautiful." She kissed her son on the cheek and embraced him tightly. "This deserves a place of prominence on the tree." Beth moved a couple of items around to put Tyler's creation front-and-center on what would be the main attraction of the Christmas decorations. "This calls for a celebration!" Beth headed to the kitchen and began to fish around one of the drawers for a spatula. "Let's dig into this divinity."

"But Mom," Tyler remembered from previous occasions, "doesn't it have to sit out for a while before we can eat it?"

"Well, it might be a bit gooey, but we can eat it now." She returned to the living room with two small plates, each containing a piece of the white fudge. Tyler, ever a lover of all things sugary, didn't need another invitation. He held the plate with his right hand and picked up the treat with his left. Placing it on his tongue, the moist contents melted into a bonanza of flavor. Tyler could only close his eyes, smile, and savor every second of the experience.

"So what do you think, Tyler? Is it good? Does it taste all right?"

"Tyler, are you enjoying it? Does it taste all right? Tyler?"

Suddenly, Tyler came to. He opened his eyes and, swallowing the divinity fudge made by his host, looked up at Jackie with a smile and said, "It's amazing."

Jackie, clearly proud of herself, said, "Oh, I am so glad! I really wanted you to enjoy that. Have you ever had divinity before?"

With a cheeky grin much like that day he presented an ornament to his mother, he said, "Yeah. A few times."

"I'm glad you enjoyed it, but the real reason I'm here is to let you know we're going to be leaving in a few minutes to head to the church. Let me take care of those things for you."

Without hesitation, Jackie threw away Tyler's plate and cup and began to gather the others for their Christmas Eve pilgrimage. Tyler stirred himself and, taking his jacket from the coat rack, reflected on what had transpired after that night of spontaneous decorating. Indeed they would be all right. Within a month, Beth had landed another office job and everything went back to normal. In retrospect, Tyler had to wonder; maybe it was his mother who actually had God's attention. Smiling once again, he put on his jacket and walked outside to unite with his fellow guests for the ride to First Community.

Six

Though he had carefully avoided much social contact at the Bennett house, it would be impossible during the ride to church. It was decided that the entire throng would commute to the church in three minivans, one of which was owned by the Bennetts and dubbed "Jackie's Ride" by Wally. It would be much more comfortable than their sedan, and the elder couple made sure Tyler would be riding in their vehicle.

In a spirit of deferment, Tyler slid open the side door and, being the youngest and spriest, automatically went to the rear of the vehicle. The minivan could seat six with each chair having its own armrests for added comfort. Being the only single in the group, Tyler knew he was going to throw off the numbering. In order to give off the impression that he was not interested in making any kind of connection, he buckled himself in and stared out the back window at nothing in particular. He had learned this tactic from the hundreds of bus trips he had taken to and from school in his young life; if you wanted to be left alone, look as unwelcoming as possible. It all came too easily to Tyler.

He knew he wouldn't have to worry about a seatmate, but he also wanted to send the message to the overenthusiastic evangelicals that he wasn't necessarily capable of matching their zeal. Within a half minute, he heard a couple walking toward the van's still-open door.

"Well lookey here, Dave! Here's a good seat right here."

"I'm comin'. I'm comin'."

"And it looks like we have some good-looking company for the ride to church."

Internally, Tyler did the equivalent of rolling his eyes as he continued looking out the window opposite from the door. The woman with far too much makeup who had made the discovery was still standing outside the vehicle as her husky husband approached and looked inside to see if he agreed with his spouse's assessment. By now, Wally and Jackie were getting situated in the front seats.

"Yoo hoo! Young man!" called the woman in hopes of catching Tyler's attention.

Tyler knew there was no turning back. He could hardly pretend to be oblivious after that kind of summons. He turned his head toward her and smiled.

Dave and Sue Kirschman had been friends of the Bennetts for many years. They had met at First Community and meshed from the outset. Dave had lived in the Greater Cleveland area his whole life. A football star in high school, the barrel-chested man was a formidable figure. A knee injury in his senior year prevented his football career from advancing to the collegiate level. At 6 feet 4 inches, the former lineman was still an imposing force in his late fifties, but this was the extent of his intimidation. About ten seconds of conversation with the man showed that he was a teddy bear through and through. He had the typical wardrobe of a former athlete, meaning he tried desperately to maintain his clothing sizes from his early twenties, though his weight painted a different picture. It was especially noticeable when Dave would sit down, and obvious gaps would open between the buttons of his dress shirt. He also made no effort to cover his expanding middle with his pants, desperately trying to retain the waist size of his playing days.

His wife Sue was the more talkative and spunkier of the two. A clear fan of tanning booths, she had a perpetual mahogany glow about her, even in the dead of winter. This sun-drenched canvas would be accentuated with matching makeup and accessories, down to the coordinated fingernail polish. She had a wonderful zest for life, and it showed in her conversational style. She worked as the main receptionist for First Community and was perfect for the role. She could talk to anyone and made all visitors feel at ease. "Could you help an old lady into the van?" she asked Tyler.

"What am I, chopped liver?" Dave said.

"It's just that I don't always get to have a young handsome man help me, that's all."

"And which part am I missing," Dave replied, "the 'young' part or the 'handsome' part?"

"I plead the Fifth," Sue resolved with a laugh. She extended her hand into the cab of the van, insisting on the help of the handsome stranger.

Tyler had no choice but to unbuckle his seatbelt and scoot toward the door. Grasping her hand, he waited for her to shift her weight upward so he could take her the rest of the way. However, it was clear that Sue was having trouble committing to lifting her other leg because of the height before her.

"All right. Give me a second, here. I don't do this as quickly as I used to," she said.

Dave inserted himself. "I have the perfect solution." Placing his hands on his wife's waist, he literally lifted her into the van, thus making Tyler's efforts completely unneeded. Once in the van, Dave couldn't help but use his right hand to pat his wife's caboose.

"Well, sir!" Sue announced as she looked back over her shoulder at her hubby, "I do believe this means we are officially courting." Sue threw her head back and laughed from her gut. Wally, adjusting the mirrors up front, let loose with one of his winsome guffaws. Jackie turned in her seat and smiled, looking at Tyler to check on him. The young man smiled playfully and shook his head. Tyler had a special place in his heart for folks a bit older with moxie. He hoped he could be like that when he was their age. The problem was that he wasn't like that at his present age.

Wally started the van, backed out of the driveway, and led the vehicle procession to the church. Tyler believed he was safe for the rest of the trip since everyone was facing the opposite direction of him. What he didn't count on was having Sue Kirschner in the same vehicle, with rotating seats.

She spun her chair about 90 degrees toward the back of the van. "So, Tyler is it?"

"Yes, ma'am," Tyler said respectfully.

"Please! Don't call me that. It makes me feel old. Just call me Sue."

"Will do."

"So is there a lovely young lady in your life?"

Wally instantly made eye contact with Tyler in his rearview mirror. Jackie did the same in the mirror of her visor. Dave took a more direct approach. "Sue! Would you please?"

"What?" Sue wondered. "What's wrong with asking a question like that? Tyler's obviously a very attractive young man. Surely he has a number of ladies who are clamoring for his attention."

"To you, the entire world is divided into two groups: Married and Not Yet."

Sue playfully swatted her husband's forearm. "Stop it! That is not how I think. You're going to make Tyler believe that all I care about is romance."

"No, you're accomplishing that all by yourself," Dave retorted.

The way Dave and Sue kept innocently dueling, all Tyler could do was turn his head back and forth as if he was watching a tennis match. He didn't know if he was one of the competitors or one of the spectators.

Dave successfully ended the volley by saying, "Let's just change the topic, shall we?"

"All right. I can take a hint," Sue said. Turning to Tyler once again, she said, "So Tyler, tell me something about yourself."

Now it had gone from a tennis match to a job interview. Tyler despised talking about himself on any level, so he was visibly discomforted by Sue's question. He looked out the window, almost hoping something he saw out of it would give him the inspiration to answer. "Well, um, I have lived in Cleveland all my life…"

"Mmmmhmmm." Sue was not going to let him simply trail off without revealing more information.

"And, uh, I am trying to be an artist."

Sue pounced on this. "More than trying! I saw the work you did for Wally and Jackie, and have to say I was very impressed." She purposely changed her voice mid-sentence to give emphasis to "very" and "impressed." Sue always used such verbal cues when communicating important information to others. While working at the church required her to handle sensitive and private information responsibly, it didn't keep her from conveying that she was privy to information others weren't. For instance, one day when the Kirschners and Bennetts were having lunch after Sunday service, Sue went into covert mode while they were eating their salads. She would lean in circumspectly and say, "Without giving any details, let's just say that Pastor Wilkins has had more than his share of high-maintenance members to deal with this week," with special emphasis on "high-maintenance" and "members." This was as revealing as Sue would get, but they found it charming.

They never pressed her for information, simply because they really didn't want to know the behind-the-scenes stories of First Community.

"Oh. Well, it's actually not one of my better efforts," Tyler offered. Among the most glaring of Tyler's social weaknesses was his inability to accept compliments properly.

After a few seconds of silence, Sue responded, "I believe the appropriate response to that compliment was, 'Thank you.'"

Tyler realized he had committed yet another social faux pas. This is why he didn't want to engage in the first place. Things like this always happened. No wonder he had no one sitting next to him in this van. Looking at the floorboard, all he could say was, "Sorry."

"No apology needed, darling. I just want you to know that I think you're very good at what you do."

Tyler neither responded nor made eye contact. He never knew what to do at such moments. He knew there was probably some deep-seated, Freudian explanation for his refusal to accept praise, but tonight was no time for deep analysis.

Sue continued to probe. "So why aren't you spending Christmas Eve with family?"

Once again, Jackie and Wally exchanged panicky glances, knowing the young man was being carried into deep waters against his will.

"Tell you what," Wally interrupted, "Why don't we go around and name our favorite and least favorite Christmas songs? Mine are 'O Holy Night' and 'Grandma Got Run Over by a Reindeer.' Jackie, how about you?"

"What? What did I say?" Sue asked while gesturing exuberantly.

Dave came to Tyler's rescue. "You'll have to excuse my wife. I'd say the punch was spiked, but she's always like this.

And Christmas seems to send her to a heightened level of excitement." He looked at his wife and raised his eyebrows, hoping she would get the hint to retreat.

"That's OK. My mom loved Christmas, too." Tyler figured this response would serve two purposes. First, it would satisfy Sue's curiosity about his family. Secondly, the use of the past tense verb would hopefully carry with it the necessary meaning.

It did. Sue smiled sheepishly and turned back toward the front. Tyler's response did more than end his conversation with the church receptionist. It ended all conversation in the van completely. No mention of favorite Christmas carols or church happenings or holidays gone by. He had innocently launched the verbal equivalent of a nuclear missile, decimating all social life within its blast zone. This served only to add more guilt to Tyler's conscience. He feared being the proverbial wet blanket on this occasion, and now his fears were being realized. Silence pervaded until Wally parked the van on the side of the downtown street and the quintet headed toward the entrance of First Community Church.

Though Tyler attended somewhat frequently, he was still largely unknown to the faithful of the congregation. As was his habit, he would purposely arrive ten minutes late and leave just as Pastor Wilkins completed his message, thus assuring no awkward conversations or moments. Now he was early. More than that, he was entering the building with the church's equivalent of celebrities. The Bennetts and Kirschners were deeply loved and respected by all. This would be the closest he had ever been to walking a red carpet anywhere.

The church building was among the most historic in Cleveland, having been built in 1841. The stone walls had endured their share of Cleveland winters and pollution. Almost a decade ago, the church had raised hundreds of thousands of dollars to sandblast a coating of dark soot that had overtaken the original color of the stone. The transformation was nothing less than spectacular, documented by the local print and news media. Tall, thick wooden doors provided almost a Gothic-like barrier to the lobby. Since the doors were also windowless, they were typically propped open on Sunday mornings rain or shine year-round. In January, the church greeters would wear leather gloves and have hot coffee at the ready to help stay warm in their service for God.

Walking up the concrete steps and crossing the threshold, the Bennetts led the way followed by the Kirschners and Tyler bringing up the rear. The greeters were greatly enthused to see their friends enter and handed them a program for the evening's events. Conversely, Tyler was treated as a first-time guest. At least twice, Tyler had to say, "No, I've actually been coming here for a while" to embarrassed volunteers. Once again, the awkwardness left by these exchanges left Tyler feeling like he should remain mute the rest of the evening. Clearly, nothing he was saying was working.

Tyler was anxious to get through the lobby and be seated in one of the back pews. He felt vulnerable out here with his social butterfly companions, fearful of another unsuspecting saint being unwittingly destroyed by his continual social missteps. Like an orbiting moon, he stayed near the two couples he traveled with but stood on the outer rim of their conversation.

Jackie, noticing his discomfort, put her arm around Tyler's waist and told the group, "Why don't we go in and have a seat before it gets too full in there?" Wally instantly picked up on her cue and held the door open leading to the sanctuary so the entire party could go in.

One of the key factors in Tyler's choosing First Community was its sense of grandeur. The ceiling was about thirty feet high. The columns holding it up were painted white and intricately carved with floral adornments. The wooden pews that lined the hundred-foot-long sanctuary were simple in their construction. No padding or frills that most churches now had. At the front were the pipes of the huge organ that was used only on special occasions like this and weddings. He privately hoped the first chord would be played at maximum volume, thus transporting him to a mystical place he desperately needed to abide this night.

Hoping he could select a seat in the sanctuary as he had done in the van, he had to be disappointed when Sue led the way to the third row then demonstratively waved the rest of them to join her. As they were seated and the prelude music continued its welcoming melody, Tyler, now between Dave Kirschner and Jackie, began looking through the program, noting the musical selections and responsive readings to come. Now that he had arrived and been seated, albeit further forward than he desired, he had to privately admit that he was glad he made it. He needed to be reminded of something higher than himself tonight. The choir, clad in red robes with white stoles, filed in professionally and was seated in the loft, just to the right of the platform. Pastor Wilkins and those participating in the service were right behind them, sitting in the large, high-back wooden chairs on the platform.

After the participants were seated on the dais, the organ suddenly stopped playing. Tyler looked up from his program and shifted his head around to see what was happening. He noticed a group of ten people wearing white dress shirts, black pants, and white gloves come in through the side door and stand behind a table with handbells of varying sizes. Each player took one in each hand and, following the director's downbeat, began the familiar refrain that is "Joy to the World."

Tyler's taste in music was much more eclectic than most his age. He was not limited to one genre but could easily traverse from popular music to jazz to classical to R&B. He loved to paraphrase Duke Ellington by saying, "There are two kinds of music in the world: good and bad." He fancied himself an admirer of good music of all kinds.

This version of "Joy to the World" was clearly in the "good" category. He marveled at the precision and glorious sound coming from the bells. He was suddenly glad to be so close to the action and be carried away by the music. To maximize his enjoyment, he decided to close his eyes and allow the melody to overtake him, four-part chimes surrounding and elevating him.

Only then did Tyler remember.

Seven

Tyler liked to tell people he was an only child…but he wasn't. In fact, he had said it for so long that he started believing it; at least, that seemed to be the only way to deal with the pain of it. Now, though, he was finally remembering things as they were.

He was five years old. To his recollection, it was the first time he would be allowed to participate in the trimming festivities. James and Beth found it to be a calculated risk, but they didn't want to wait another twelve months until their firstborn could be a part of the celebration Christmas had become in the Ramsey house. For weeks, Tyler had been begging to help, with innumerable variations of "Please, Mom and Dad? Please?" And as Thanksgiving approached, two blessings awaited him: the aforementioned decorating and the arrival of his baby brother.

It seemed only right that Mrs. Ramsey should have a baby at Christmastime. Her due date was December 15. While some couples enjoyed being coy about the gender of their soon-to-be, James and Beth wanted the whole world to know. They also readily expressed their glee at his near-Christmas due date. They had already named him Christopher, with a middle name to be decided on closer to the birth. Tyler kept pushing for "Santa," but his parents wouldn't even entertain the thought.

Due to his dad's work schedule, Tyler was informed that the decorating would be delayed from its usual time, Thanksgiving weekend. December 1 would be the day of transformation. With the energy that comes from being a kindergartener, the playful boy in anticipation would regularly jump up and down for no reason and yell, "I can't wait! I can't wait! I can't wait!" He always said it three times in succession, making his mother laugh. Beth said she had purchased a couple of new ornaments for the occasion and would reveal them on the day they decorated. Tyler couldn't stand being outside the information loop, so he peppered his mother with questions about what they could be. His thirst for information only fueled his mother's fire to not tell him. They were both headstrong, and it showed at playful moments like this.

All of that changed on November 27.

That afternoon, Tyler was surprised to have his neighbor Mrs. Birnbaum picking him up from school. She appeared at the classroom door and the young student was called over by his teacher. "Tyler, Mrs. Birnbaum is going to take you home today, OK?" Apparently, everything had been pre-arranged with everyone but him. Tyler nodded suspiciously. It's not that he didn't like Mrs. Birnbaum. She was a sweet widow and helped out in a pinch when his parents couldn't find a sitter. However, this seemed above and beyond the call. Violet Birnbaum buckled her precious cargo into the back seat, started the car, and made the familiar drive back to their street.

"So what's going on? Where's Mom?" Tyler, like most five-year-olds, usually took the direct approach.

Casually, without missing a beat, his chauffeur said, "Nothing. Your mom got tied up with something and I offered to help."

"How come Dad couldn't do it? Is he working?"

"Well, he was, but now he's with your mother." Violet realized she had already said too much and added nothing further.

That wasn't about to satisfy the curiosity of a little boy with an active imagination. "Where are they? Are you driving me to meet them?"

"No, Tyler. You're going to stay at my house for a while."

Tyler let out a faint "humph." None of this was making sense, but he decided to go with the flow. "Oh, OK. Do you have TV at your house?"

"Sure do."

"Cool! Can I watch cartoons?"

For the first time during this transport, Violet was relieved. "Absolutely. Whatever you like."

The next few hours went without incident as Tyler plunged himself headlong into the antics of animated characters and their hijinks. By 7 p.m., however, he was getting concerned. During a commercial break, he got up from the floor in front of the television and strolled into the kitchen where Violet was balancing her checkbook. "Hey!" Tyler could be a bit pushy when he felt out of control, even at this young age. "Where's my mom? When's she coming back?"

Violet was clearly devising a Plan B. She had obviously been under orders to not tell Tyler the whole story, but she couldn't keep this charade up any longer. It wasn't fair to him. She picked him up and put him on her lap. Tyler was visibly surprised by the gesture as Mrs. Birnbaum had not shown much affection to this point. "Tyler, you probably should know that your mom is in the hospital."

"Is she having the baby right now?"

"Yes, but the baby is earlier than expected."

"That's OK. We're ready for him."

"No, I don't mean that, sweetie. I mean that Christopher wasn't ready."

Tyler was no grammar expert, but the use of the word "wasn't" caught his young mind's attention. "So, what's wrong?"

Violet was at a complete loss. This was hard to discuss with another adult, let alone making it understandable and palatable for a five-year-old. "Well, something went wrong. Christopher was born early and wasn't breathing when he came out. The doctors did everything they could…"

"So, is my brother in heaven now, Mrs. Birnbaum?"

A slight smile briefly crossed Violet's lips. "Yes, Tyler. I think that's exactly where he is."

Tyler didn't really cry. How much of life and death can be comprehended at that age? It is hard to grieve over someone you have never met, and he seemed comforted by the thought of him being with Jesus, just like his Sunday School teacher had talked about one time. "So is my Mom coming here to pick me up?"

"No, not tonight. They'll probably keep her there tonight to make sure she's feeling all right."

Tyler exhaled loudly. "OK. Well, I guess I'll just watch some more cartoons."

"All right, honey, but I'll make us some dinner. I'll call you when it's ready."

Tyler didn't really know how to feel. He would probably wait to talk to his parents to get more understanding about what just happened. He truly didn't know if it was good or bad. I mean, heaven is the place to be, right? Shouldn't Tyler be happy about that?

About 30 minutes later, Tyler and Violet had a bowl of beef stew – not Tyler's favorite dish (especially when thick carrots were present), but he knew better than to ask for something else. As they were finishing, the glare of headlights appeared in the kitchen window and both occupants at the table knew that James had pulled into the driveway. Exiting his car, he walked to the unlocked back door, gave a polite tap and opened it, revealing his son and charitable neighbor.

"Daddy!" Tyler was so glad to see one of his parents that he leaped from his dining room chair and sprinted to his father. The boy was surprised to discover that his father's enthusiasm nowhere near matched his own. He could see it in his face and even in the way he embraced him, if you could call it an embrace. Something wasn't there that was there before. "Get your stuff, Tyler," his father ordered and promptly walked out the door without so much as greeting their son's caretaker. Violet arose from her chair and helped the young man reassemble the contents of his backpack and put on his winter coat.

Just before going out the back door, Tyler turned to his emergency host and said, "Thanks, Mrs. Birnbaum!" Violet put her hands to her mouth, overcome by the emotion of the moment and the kindness exhibited by someone so young.

Years later, in the rare moments he permitted himself to ponder such things, Tyler would reason that it was that specific night in which he lost his father. As they pulled away from the Birnbaum house, James could only stare at the road before him. Tyler could feel the tension and wasn't sure why his dad appeared so sullen. He knew he needed to make his father feel better. "Dad, Mrs. Birnbaum told me about Christopher. I'm glad he's in heaven now."

This would be the first and only time that Tyler would ever see his father cry. Tears began streaming down his face, and he began to whimper. With one hand, he would hold the steering wheel and use the opposite sleeve to wipe his eyes and nose. It was all he could do to maintain some semblance of control over the vehicle.

"It's OK, Daddy. He's with Jesus now."

"Be quiet! Just keep your mouth shut for once!" his father yelled at the top of his lungs, glaring at him in the rearview mirror. From its volume, the intended target was more above James than behind him, but Tyler didn't know that. The boy leaned his head forward, closed his eyes, and began crying. Most fathers would have instantly recognized their misdeed and immediately tried to rectify it. But James was past caring. The best he could muster was silence. As his still living son cried quietly, James pulled into the Ramsey driveway, shut off the car, exited the vehicle, unlocked the front door of the house, and slammed it behind him, leaving his weeping son still buckled into the back seat. Tyler remained there for a while, unsure of why he sustained such a wounding. He eventually managed to unbuckle himself and leave the car (though it was difficult for him to open the door wide enough). Arriving on the front porch, he reached up slightly for the handle and slowly turned the knob. Upon entry, he pushed it closed, secured the lock, and waited in the entryway.

He didn't see or hear his father. The only light he could make out was underneath the master bedroom door. He knew better than to knock, as he didn't want a repeat of the trip home. He made his way down the hall and headed for his room. Just before reaching it, however, he walked past the nursery that had been dedicated to Christopher. It had already been painted by his mother with his name in calligraphy on the wall. All the accoutrements were in place, including a baby swing, exer-saucer, and changing bed. Tyler wondered what would happen to all of it. He entered his room and eventually fell asleep without so much as a "Good night" from his father.

Beth would come home the next day. Tyler stayed home from school, as his house was empty when he awoke. It was a good thing Tyler was an introvert, as this would be a jolting experience for anyone to endure. Still clad only in underwear, he stumbled to the kitchen, grabbed a box of cereal and went to the living room to watch cartoons and eat his breakfast staple without milk.

Just after noon, the car pulled back in and his father assisted his mother from the car and into the house. Seeing his mother made Tyler quickly forget the reason for her absence and he darted toward her to welcome her back home. As he neared, she held out her hand to keep him at bay and said, "Be careful, sweetheart. Mommy's still sore." Once again, Tyler had been rebuffed. Even less patient, James barked at him, "Go get dressed, Tyler, and let your mother get some rest." In frustration, Tyler ran to his room, slammed the door behind him, flung himself on the bed, and cried in his pillow. It seemed to be the only thing he could run to.

As December 1st neared, the family's enthusiasm level was at an all-time low. Tyler's "I can't wait" chant had been silenced. No mention of Christmas had even been made, let alone boxes of decorations being delivered from the attic. Randomly at meals over those few days, Beth would begin to sob uncontrollably. Initially, James tried to console her; but he eventually came to the point of being in a catatonic state. All Tyler could wonder was whether it was his fault. Maybe he was the one who had caused all this tension. His only relief seemed to be in front of the television.

On the morning of Saturday the 1st, Tyler emerged from his bedroom to find his parents sitting quietly in the living room. James was reading the Sports section of the local newspaper while his mother was looking out the front window.

With all the courage he could summon, Tyler asked both of them, "Do you think we'll put up the Christmas tree today?"

James immediately scowled at him for even bringing up the subject. "Tyler! We don't need to deal with that right now." He folded his current page with emphasis and went back to his previous place.

Tyler was downcast. He was disappointed that he wouldn't finally be able to help. He couldn't figure out why everyone was so sad. Wasn't heaven supposed to be the best place anywhere? That's what everyone, including his parents, had told him when their pet kitten died the year before. They said it's where they were all going someday. So now, why was it suddenly so bad? Maybe he really had done something to mess everything up.

Beth then turned her head toward her son and said, "No, that's OK. We need to. It will be a nice distraction."

Tyler couldn't help himself. He squealed in delight and jumped around in a circle with complete abandon. He then began doing a celebratory dance like he had seen football players do on TV while watching games with his dad, yelling, "Oh yeah! Oh yeah! We're gonna put up the tree. Oh yeah!" His mother smiled for the first time in almost a week. At that moment, Beth Ramsey realized how close she came to losing both of her children.

Unfortunately, James never made that journey. His look of disdain for the project could not be obscured. He glared at his innocent son, unhappy that the day would be filled with remembrance and joy. For him, all joy had escaped. No, more than that; it had been taken away from him. There would be no festivity. There would be no gaiety. To him, a contract had been broken, and he deserved reparations. Grudgingly, however, he went along with the order of the day and brought down all the large boxes of decorations. From there, he retreated to the bedroom while Beth began organizing all the knick-knacks and tree necessities.

Tyler was a good helper and stayed on task, even when the initial enthusiasm wore off. Beth always admired his stick-to-itiveness. She remembered him as a one-year-old, stacking blocks as high as he could. He would always be able to do three, but the fourth would always send the structure tumbling down. He would cry and scream out of frustration, but instead of abandoning the task would come back to it until he could finally get four. All through the day, Tyler continually said, "What next, Mom? What's next?" Beth was never flustered by his constant need to know. She was careful to celebrate his passions, realizing that what he loved to do now would be what he loved to do later, if she reinforced him properly.

Occasionally, James would show himself, but only on his way to and from the fridge. He had turned on the bedroom television and was watching college football in there. His sporadic trips were strictly for purposes of renewing supplies. Rather than be offended at his absence, Tyler was relieved. He had only been in his father's crosshairs since that fateful night, and he was grateful for a reprieve.

Afternoon transitioned into evening, and with it came the final task of the day: putting on the ornaments. Beth wouldn't allow James to sit this part out. She went to the bedroom, peaked her head in, said something Tyler couldn't discern, and trotted back to the living room.

"Ready Mom?" Tyler asked.

"Not quite yet. We need to wait for Daddy."

The boy was disheartened with that news; but when his mother spoke authoritatively like that, there was no further discussion. They waited for about five minutes while instrumental Christmas music played on the family CD player. To fill the time, Beth began singing along with the trumpeted fanfare. "Glory to the newborn King. Peace on earth and mercy mild…" Though having no concept of what the lyrics were, Tyler wasn't about to let that stop him from joining in chorus with his mom. His version sounded more like, "Wowy oooo a oooo ing!" By the time the song finished, James had taken his seat in the large stuffed chair but didn't put his feet on the ottoman in case he was needed.

And he was. Beth would not allow him to simply observe. With the precision of an air traffic controller, she instructed her husband and son on which ornaments to hang and where, all while doing the same herself. It was a sight to behold and truth be known the part of the day Tyler looked forward to the most. Occasionally, some repositioning would have to be done so that ornaments of varying colors were rightly apportioned. "OK, Dad, let's take that gold one here and put it on the other side." "Tyler, we're a little bare down here at the bottom. Let's have you put the elf there." And so it went until every usable ornament was removed and hung. Had it not been for the underlay of Christmas music, there would have been palpable tension throughout the process.

"What do you think?" Beth asked. "Should we turn off the lights and see how it looks?"

James said nothing, but Tyler's fertile mind suddenly recalled something. "No wait! Not yet! We have to put up the new ornaments you bought, Mommy! Where are they? What are they?" A new burst of excited energy ran through the boy, but his father leaned back in his chair so that his head was against the headrest. Even Beth couldn't help but look down that time. The young lad could only wonder what he had said that was so awful. Why was he causing so much pain?

His mother wiped discernible tears from her eyes and walked toward the hallway closet. James covered his eyes in obvious grief. She returned with a small manufacturer's box which contained two new but identical ornaments. Braving her emotions, Beth put her hand on Tyler's shoulder and said, "Well sweetie, a while ago your dad and I were out shopping and we saw a clearance bin at the department store. They were selling things from last Christmas that no one had bought but at a much lower price. Knowing I was pregnant with your brother, I saw these ornaments and thought they would be perfect for the tree this year." The box contained two silver (actually tin) bells. They even had small clappers inside that caused the bell to ring when jostled. "We wanted the two bells to represent our two children, you and Christopher."

That was all James could stand. With his right foot, he pushed the ottoman across the living room floor. As he stood from the chair and stomped toward the bedroom again, he snarled at Tyler, "Stupid kid! Just couldn't leave well enough alone!" He slammed the master bedroom door with such force that a hallway picture on the opposite wall fell to the floor.

Tyler once again hung his head in shame. Everything seemed to be his fault. He didn't know what he had done or said this time, but he was beginning to think that silence might be his best friend from this point forward. Beth was still wiping tears from her eyes when her son asked, "Why are you so sad, Mommy? Isn't Christopher in heaven?"

Beth brought her son on the couch next to her, stroked his hair, and said, "Yes, he certainly is; but I have to admit that I wanted to get to know him the way I've gotten to know and love you. I wanted him to decorate the tree with us and for you two to ride bikes together and play baseball together. I know he belongs to Jesus, but I wanted him for myself a little bit, too."

"So did I!" Tyler announced.

"I know, sweetie. It's just going to take me a little while to get used to his not being here. Does that make sense?" Tyler nodded his head but didn't say anything. It really didn't make sense. He was disappointed at not having a little brother, but he couldn't possibly relate to the anger and anguish being experienced by his father and mother, respectively.

"Is Daddy going to be mad at me for a while?"

"He's not really mad at you. I think he will come around," is all Beth said. She quickly changed the subject. "Tell you what. Why don't we put those bell ornaments on the tree and see how it looks; what do you say?"

Tyler approached the tree and hung both bells where his mother had indicated. He pointed to the second and final one, saying, "This one is for Christopher." He even took the liberty of ringing it with his thumb and index finger moving it back and forth. "Yay, Christopher! Merry Christmas!" Tyler said robustly.

Tears returned to Beth's eyes, as she enthusiastically repeated Tyler's refrain. She couldn't have thought of a more moving tribute to her departed son. She turned off the living room lights, returned her son to his position next to her on the sofa, and said, "Isn't it beautiful, sweetheart?" The little boy nodded with his usual sense of wonder as he surveyed his craftsmanship for the very first time. Beth looked down at him, appreciative that through all the horrific events of the last week, her son had not lost the sense of delight that had constantly accompanied him his whole life. She prayed he would never lose it. "How 'bout we sing some more?"

"OK, Mom. You go first." This was Tyler's creative way of saying, "I don't know the words."

Beth giggled and said, "All right." She listened to the instrumental music to discern what part of the song it could have been then jumped in. "And heaven and nature sing – and heaven and nature sing…"

Suddenly a boisterous chorus of congregation and handbells sounded out the final notes, "And heaven, and heaven, and nature sing!" While all faces around were filled with delight, a much older Tyler was experiencing something else. It wasn't great, but it wasn't terrible either. Tears came to his eyes as he thought about those events for the first time in many years. Not wanting to draw attention to himself, he wiped his tears with his thumb and middle finger on either eye. His sniff prompted Jackie to sneak a tissue from her purse into Tyler's hand. As he made his necessary adjustments, Jackie took mind to grab his other hand and not let go.

For some people, finding the right church is an arduous task. For Tyler, it was even more daunting. Purely as a reaction to his negative experiences as a teenager, he wanted somewhere a bit more formal than he had known. However, he didn't want something so formal that there was no sense of life in the place. "Starchy" is what Tyler called it. He wanted something exciting and relevant but not out of control. Finding that balance became a bit of a task. Truth be known, when he first moved into his apartment, he went to church only to satisfy his mother. She was worried he would be spiritually adrift without it. What Tyler never had the heart to tell her was how, even with it, life felt like an unending voyage on an inflatable raft.

First Community was the fourth and final church he examined. While he appreciated the friendliness and the ministries of the church, it was Pastor Roger Wilkins who really sold him. His sermons were the most timely and pertinent messages he had ever heard. He had that remarkable ability to look into Tyler's soul and say what needed to be said to keep him afloat for another week. The young artist was long past being impressed with church gimmicks and slick marketing ideas. He was a "meat and potatoes" guy; meaning he just wanted the scriptural truth presented in a professional manner. When he made it through the doors, he never walked away disappointed.

He wished he had the resolve to make it every Sunday, but he often worked the Saturday evening shift, as that was the time to make the best tips. He wouldn't get home until well after midnight and not arise until about noon on Sunday. Sometimes, he would be asked to work the Sunday lunch shift, which was also the time to make the absolute worst tips…when the church people were let loose on the area's restaurants. In food service, Tyler had seen a completely different side of church life, and it wasn't always pretty. They were sometimes the most demanding and least appreciative of all his customers. Drunken patrons were easier to handle and certainly better tippers than the "Christian crowd," as his co-workers called them. He recoiled when they would pray before their meal – not because he was ashamed of prayer, but because any subsequent obnoxiousness would ultimately hurt the cause of Christianity.

Tyler was patient as occasional guests would try to present him with the gospel and lead him to Christ. He would lean in and tell the party that he was already a Christian. What surprised him was how quickly they lost interest after that and treated him more like a serf than a server. That or someone at the table would doubt his claims. "Well, everyone likes to say they're a Christian nowadays," they would respond, "but do you really believe in Jesus?" Tyler would again assert his personal faith in Christ and sometimes still not be believed. He wondered if the Inquisition had somehow resurfaced without his knowing it.

However, the best of all, Tyler rendered, were the tract tippers. These hearty souls would demand constant refills and continuous free bread and leave a gospel tract instead of a tip upon their departure. Tyler's personal favorite was the tract made to look like a $20 bill. Though not Catholic, the young waiter wondered if purgatory could exist for these people alone.

As the service continued this Christmas Eve, Tyler once again resolved that in the new year he was going to make a renewed commitment to be in church regardless of how tired he was. He knew that attending was always a good decision, so whatever inconvenience was posed in the morning, he could resolve in the afternoon with a nap.

Through the responsive readings, choir songs, and congregational carols, Tyler would look at his program to see what was coming next. It was an odd habit of Tyler's. He had this undying curiosity always to know what was next and not be caught off-guard. When Pastor Wilkins had a handout for his Sunday messages with blanks, Tyler had to discipline himself to listen to what his pastor was saying, rather than occupying his thoughts guessing what would go in the blanks. He had to remember he was in church, not on a game show. He was greatly anticipating Pastor Roger's message and wondered what he would have up his sleeve for Christmas. The program contained the title of his message, "Far from Home." The young worshiper tried to reckon where he was going with the title. Maybe he was referring to Jesus leaving His place in heaven to accomplish His ultimate mission. Again, he had to rouse himself and remember to stay in the moment. He would find out soon enough.

He noticed an eight-foot table to the left of the pulpit. On it were three distinct items, but all covered with a red tablecloth. Apparently, this was going to be part of the message. Occasionally, Tyler would look at the table, trying to predict what could be underneath. He was the same way as a child at Christmas. Rather than waiting for the moment of joy Christmas morning, he would study each present under the tree and try to deduce what was in each box. He started to get so good at it that Beth would wait until the last possible moment to put out the gifts so as not to ruin the surprise.

As he surveyed the mysterious table, he could almost hear Beth say, "Tyler, would you just wait and enjoy the moment?" He decided to take her posthumous advice and focus on the service at hand.

After singing "Angels We Have Heard on High" as a congregation, they remained standing as Pastor Wilkins took to the pulpit to read the text for his message. Roger Wilkins was in his mid-fifties, sported mostly white hair, and always wore his trademark glasses. Everything about him looked polished. He was the essence of professional, which was very important for the clientele of this congregation. Business people could attend here and bring their friends knowing they would have a good experience. In an age where most churches were trending to more casual dress for their clergy, Roger was a suit-and-tie guy. Wally once commented that, had the ministry not been his calling, he would have made a great lawyer. He just looked the part. He was quite distinguished, having no trace of arrogance in his preaching. It was quite common for Wilkins to tell stories on himself, especially ones in which he didn't play the hero. It was rare to hear such authenticity from a pastor of such importance.

Tyler wished he had the courage to meet him, but he was intimidated by most men in authority. Maybe he was just afraid that connecting with him socially would ruin the image he had of him spiritually. One thing was certain: He had nothing but true respect for this man and wanted nothing to taint it.

Wearing a well-tailored black suit with red tie and white kerchief, Pastor Wilkins read from Matthew chapter 2 and the journey of the wise men, first to King Herod, then to the young child named Jesus. He asked the congregation to be seated after he finished reading his text and began to speak about the Wise Men who have become such a large part of Christmas lore. He spoke of many of the misconceptions that we have of them; that we're not sure how many of them there were, that we assume three because of the three gifts that were given; that they didn't travel alone, but more resembled an entourage including assistants and servants to tend to the many needs of such a long journey; that they didn't come from the Orient as depicted in the famous hymn, but more than likely originated from Persia or Mesopotamia. These are the kinds of things Tyler loved to learn in church. He loved it when speakers could deconstruct myths and old wives' tales about the Bible and get at the essential truths in Scripture. Pastor Wilkins did it better than anyone else.

He then began a biographical treatise of the Magi, hoping for the audience to empathize with the sacrifice they had made. "Think of what these men did. They were so dedicated both to their astronomical and theological studies that they had to explore what happens at the intersecting point between the two of them." Tyler had never thought of it that way before, that God had literally brought heaven and earth together in that magical moment.

"They cared little for their own convenience. To embark on such a journey would test the limits of their dedication and belief. They did not know how long it would take, how much supplies to bring along, or how far they would go. All they knew was that they were to go. Isn't that the mark of almost every great man or woman in Scripture? They are confronted with something beyond themselves, and that something eventually becomes the heartbeat of their life. Everything else becomes secondary to the mission they know they have received from Almighty God.

"When Abraham was told to leave the land of safety and security and journey to a place he had never seen before, he went far away from home; and he did it with joy because of Who was calling him. When Noah was given specific instructions by the Lord to prepare a structure that had never been seen or utilized to that point in man's history, he did so joyfully in spite of the taunts and insults; and the rains came and took him far from home until they came to rest on Ararat to begin anew. When Joseph placed himself in God's hands, he was the victim of an awful plot that sent him into slavery and later prison, far from home; but it was where God wanted him to be and he became a man of great influence because of his trust in God.

"On this Christmas Eve, you may feel far from home as well. Perhaps you have followed God to the best of your ability, but you feel stranded and even abandoned on your journey."

That resonated with Tyler. Once again, his pastor had done it: reached into his heart and pulled it out for introspective examination. He not only felt far from home; he didn't know where home was anymore. He lowered his head and began looking at his program while hanging on every word from the speaker.

"These Magi were far from home too. They had traveled hundreds of miles in the hope of seeing someone they believed would be important someday. Doing so put them at risk from bandits, thieves, and political tyrants like Herod. It was a perilous journey, and at times they had to wonder if their dreams masked their nightmares."

Tyler felt almost singled out now. He wondered if Wally or Jackie had called Roger in advance to tell him the young man's plight, even suggesting sermon material to help him. That's how much of a setup the whole thing felt. But he knew better. He knew Someone else was at work tonight. He just didn't know how.

"Another misconception we have about the Wise Men is that they arrived the night of Christ's birth, when in fact they arrived months later. Some even wonder if Jesus was two years old at the time, because Herod ordered all boys 2 and under to be slaughtered in an effort to keep Biblical prophecy from being fulfilled. Yet, after all those months of travel through desert and danger, they arrived to find an infant, and a plain-looking one at that."

The crowd giggled a bit if for no other reason than to break the tension. This was no time-filler message for the saints. Pastor Wilkins was on a mission, and everyone knew it.

"How did they know this baby would be anything or do anything? Truth is they didn't. All they did was follow God and believe. Contrary to the paintings we see of Jesus as a baby, there wasn't a perpetual spotlight or halo on Him, indicating His deity or majesty. He was just a plain kid who cooed, cried, and spit up.

"Still, all of their study and all of their learning and all of their faith had led to this one moment. They would choose to believe that their journey had meant something. Think of this: They probably would not even be alive to see the fulfillment of it 30-plus years later. On this side of heaven, they would never even know if their journey that sent them far from home was worth it – except for their belief.

"That's what you and I face on this Christmas Eve night. Every day we are journeying through this life and through this world trying to make sense of the ups and downs of it. We are desperately trying to believe in something we can't see in spite of those who tell us we worship folklore and fairy tales. At times, we wonder what it's all about and whether it's worth it when we consider the heartbreak and losses that accompany this life."

It was all Tyler could do to keep his composure. Growing up in the Pentecostal church, a parishioner going through this experience would use the expression, "He's reading my mail!" It seemed Pastor Wilkins had crafted this message for him. Tyler began this night as an exercise of going through the Christmas motions. Now he couldn't deny that he had a rendezvous pre-appointed for him in this place.

"I want you to know that, if God has called you, the journey is worth it, even when He calls us far from home to accomplish it. The journey is worth it because of Who is at the end of the journey. You see, when we examine the truth of Scripture, we are all far away from home tonight. Oh, we may be gathered with family and friends and practicing our annual holiday traditions, but this is not our home. Our real home is heaven, and Jesus is preparing a place for us there. We are far from home, but we are not left without purpose. We have something we can give, an act we can perform, a gift we can share that will transform lives."

Tyler thought about his art and was renewed with enthusiasm for what it could potentially bring to people. He remembered that he was not left unequipped for his life but still had plenty to share with humanity. He was glad to be reminded that his path was not pointless. Still, he could not shake the feeling of isolation that overwhelmed him.

"When the Wise Men and traveling party arrived to meet Joseph, Mary, and the Anointed Messiah, they brought gifts that would exemplify what He would accomplish on the earth." Now Pastor Wilkins strolled elegantly toward the covered table on the left. This would be the Big Reveal that Tyler had awaited. Removing the top cloth, he unveiled three items that no doubt represented the three gifts of the Magi. On the far left was an object no doubt made to look like a large bar of gold. With an artist's eye, Tyler could quickly tell that it had been spray-painted with gold lacquer to give it that appearance. An actual gold bar of that size would have bankrupted the church budget. In the middle of the display was a large silver dish filled with some sort of substance. Even from the front of the church, he couldn't tell if it was sand, ash, or soil. Coming out from that substance was a handful of large sticks, looking like extremely tall candles on a birthday cake. On the far right was a brown-colored translucent bottle of what appeared to be oil. It looked reminiscent of the vials of anointing oil that the elders would use at his old church when they prayed for sick people.

Far from being a church novice, Tyler quickly deduced that these represented gold, frankincense, and myrrh. However, to assume that he knew where his pastor was going with them would be to greatly underestimate Roger's ability to put a new spin on a familiar story.

"Each gift was more symbolic than pragmatic to this young family." He picked up the fake gold bar and continued. "Gold is an indication of kingship, power, and security. It was meant to depict that He is the King of Kings and Lord of Lords. However, his kingship would not be realized in His earthly life the way many hoped. No, because of His death and resurrection, He became the ruler of an invisible kingdom that has no borders or limits. He has set up His kingdom within us. Wherever we go, the Kingdom goes; and Jesus rules and reigns over all of us. We are His loyal, loving, and willing servants."

Tyler loved the way Pastor Wilkins could put a sentence together. It was Biblically truthful but almost lyrical in content. The oratory elevated his thinking and processing. He couldn't help looking on either side of him at his dinner companions. They seemed to sense it, too. Their countenances shone with the beauty of each word. As Roger continued to speak about gold, specifically the gold that awaited all believers in heaven, Tyler could sense his thoughts and ambitions becoming loftier with every word. He didn't want to miss a word of it.

Wilkins put down the faux gold bar and walked behind the table to the center. There sat the bowl with large sticks anchored in the foreign substance. Taking a nearby lighter, he lit each of the sticks. Immediately, they began to smolder and a subtle smoke began to rise and permeate the room. Tyler had smelled incense before and truthfully wasn't a fan. In spite of all the scriptures mentioning it, particularly in the tabernacle and later the temple in Jerusalem, Tyler was grateful to be living in a later era in which it was rarely used. To him, the aroma usually smelled like an odd mix of cinnamon cookies and gym socks. He anticipated the worst and braced himself for the pungent wallop he was about to take.

Pastor Wilkins continued, "Frankincense was obtained from the Boswellia tree found primarily in the Middle East. Typically, the bark would be scraped away. Then the surface of the tree would be struck with a tap or a spike so that it penetrated deep into the innards of the tree. This would cause a sap to emerge on the surface. It was an inner resin that would eventually harden into a gum-like substance that could be burned. It was said that the scent from it was so refreshing that it could heal people of depression and mental difficulties."

Tyler had never heard this before, but it fascinated him.

"This would serve as a sign of the death that Jesus would undergo. His body would be penetrated by whips, thorns, and nails. He would be deeply struck and tapped. However, what came to the surface, His precious blood, is now what brings forgiveness of sins, healing for our bodies, and transformation of our souls. That, my friend, is the kind of love the Father has for His children. He spared nothing; no expense was too high. He thought you were worth it. He allowed Himself to be penetrated and beaten beyond recognition so that we could experience true freedom and forgiveness today."

The young man was overwhelmed. A story he had heard hundreds of times was taking on greater significance. As if Christmas hadn't already played a large role in his life, that role was now expanding. At that moment, the smoke from the incense arrived at the third row of First Community Church, and what Tyler smelled was quite surprising. Instead of the incense he had endured in other ceremonial gatherings, this had a much more pleasant scent to it. He didn't know if it was actual frankincense or a decision from leadership to make the perfume more tolerable to the audience. Either way, it was enchanting. It had a clean smell to it, but not something antiseptic that one would smell at a hospital or nursing home. No, this had a distinct scent of pine that was quite predominant and pleasing. Tyler closed his eyes and enjoyed the feast of senses he was experiencing in this service.

It was only then that Tyler remembered.

Nine

James Ramsey had gone from having two children to none; at least, that was the impression left upon his family. Having been melancholic at his best, his wife's miscarriage the year before had plunged the young father into a steep descent of depression and emotional malaise.

James hadn't received the necessary love and skills from his parents in his formative years. Like many men of his generation, Jack Ramsey was not known for his affection. A veteran who had experienced more than his share of combat, Jack was more seen than heard in the family home. When he did speak, however, one could rest assured it was for the express purpose of administering justice. His methods of discipline, at best, could be described as strict, and, at worst, abusive. He did not tolerate insubordination (his word, due to his military experience), especially when it came to the children attempting to undermine his wife Claire. At the slightest hint of his kids lying or back-talking their mother, consequences would be felt, literally. He always did so in the throes of anger, usually on their backside but on occasion wherever his hand or fist happened to make first contact.

Every few months, usually during a drive in the car without her husband present, Claire would try to defend his tactics and use phrases like, "Your father is trying his best. He's just been through a lot in his life." These weren't so much conversations as dysfunctional press releases in which feedback wasn't invited. Out of earshot, the kids took to calling their dad

"Sarge" and had little to no love for him or his ways. Their mother was clearly the velvet glove of the relationship, and the children always felt more comfortable with her, though the bar had been set rather low. This was how the first three Ramsey children experienced life.

James was a surprise pregnancy; a welcome one for Claire, but not for Jack. He would be born ten years after his nearest sibling, Sally. By the time James had reached elementary school, his two sisters and brother had moved out of the house, Carol and Tom attending college in Virginia and Texas, respectively. Sally had carried on the family tradition in the military by enlisting in the Air Force and being stationed at Fort Eglin in Florida. Though too young to realize it at the time, James would later surmise that the kids seemingly couldn't get far enough from their Cleveland home.

Time and a greater cultural awareness of child abuse had seemingly mellowed out Jack. However, what the middle-aged man lacked in wrath he more than made up for in emotional distance. Rather early in his life, James could sense that he was more of an unwelcome houseguest than a cherished son. Jack neither struck nor ridiculed him; he just didn't do anything. His fourth child was a non-entity, an unwanted obstacle to an empty nest. While the elder children constantly felt the explosive tension of his hair-trigger temper, James was left to suffer in silence. Dinners at home typically involved Claire peppering James with questions about his day while the patriarch busily chewed and swallowed his meal without participating in the conversation. While his mother did what she could to compensate for her husband's lack of interest, "Jimmy," as he was called, looked for ways to gain his father's attention.

Sports seemed to provide the best potential for praise. Jack would dutifully watch all kinds of sports on television. He was passionate about the Cleveland Indians and Browns and spent most Sundays coaching from his recliner while he watched his favorite teams. From his authoritative and boisterous comments, he seemed to know what he was talking about. Maybe this could be common ground. Jimmy's earliest years were spent playing soccer on Saturdays without his father attending, decreeing it "wasn't a real American sport."

The young boy quickly shifted his focus to Little League baseball in the summers of his elementary school days. However, being the starting shortstop and having one of the highest hitting percentages in the league was not enough to get his father to occupy a spot in the bleachers for any of his contests. Before each game, James would undergo the same horrific ritual. While he took batting practice and later fielded grounders during warm-ups, he would invariably look behind the chain link fencing that surrounded the home plate and dugout areas, scanning the rows for Jack Ramsey. Each time, his search would end when he spotted his mother unaccompanied on one of the lower bleachers wearing sunglasses and keeping her purse at her side.

When he got to high school, he thought football would be the perfect way to capture his father's elusive approval. After all, in Cleveland, high school football is a cultural event, a natural gathering place for everyone in the community. He thought his father would show up, if for no other reason than to be seen. It didn't work. Even starting as a defensive back as a sophomore on the varsity team was not enough to lure him out of the shadows. Much like she had done in the past, Claire felt the compulsion to explain her spouse's behavior when Jimmy seemed at his lowest. "You know, your father hates missing your games, but he has so much to do." James wouldn't argue; he could only angrily ponder the idea that his father had greater loyalty to television shows than to him.

Immediately following his sophomore season, James decided to pursue one of his personal interests for a change. He always had an interest in acting and performing before a live audience but never had the opportunity to develop it. Hearing about tryouts for the spring musical, "The Music Man," the neophyte auditioned for a number of parts and was shocked to discover that he had been chosen to play Professor Harold Hill, the lead and namesake of the production. Since it is a demanding role, the director/drama teacher suggested that he watch a video of the film, so he could familiarize himself with the songs and style of the musical. He managed to find a copy at the local library and, upon arriving home that afternoon, began watching it in the living room.

About an hour into the film, his father arrived home. What the elder heard emanating from the living room disturbed him. He furrowed his brow and marched into the living room. As a "man's man," Jack made sure that the only song heard on the Ramsey television was the National Anthem immediately before the start of whatever sports event he was watching. The last thing he anticipated was hearing "Marian the Librarian" in his house after a long day at work.

"What's this supposed to be?" Jack growled.

"Huh? Oh, it's 'The Music Man'," James answered.

"And why is this crap playing in my living room?"

James was immediately on the defensive. It was rare that he and his father engaged in conversation, and he wasn't sure if what was now taking place could be put under that heading. "I have to watch it – for school." James was doing all he can to not lie to his father but also not tell him the whole truth.

"For what class? What in the world are they teaching you over there at that school?"

James didn't respond, hoping it was more of a rhetorical question. For once, he was actually hoping for his father to launch into one of his notorious "back in my day" monologues in which stark contrasts would be made between his generation and the present one, thus getting him off subject and ultimately leaving James alone. It wasn't to be.

"I said, 'For what class?'" Jack's temper was making itself known as it hadn't in some time.

"It's for Drama."

"Drama?" his father barked. "What kind of a pansy class is that?"

There really was no turning back for James now. Like a motor home in the path of a cyclone, all he could do was bear the brunt of whatever maelstrom was headed his way and pray he was still standing when it was over. "Well, it's not for a drama class but a drama production. This spring, the school is going to perform 'The Music Man,' and I was chosen to play the lead character. Pretty cool, huh?"

"Well I don't think so!" Jack yelled. He walked over and shut off the movie, along with the television playing it. He returned to the couch, standing directly over his youngest, applying maximum intimidation. James almost had to look straight up to see him. It was as if he were sitting on the front row of a movie theater, overwhelmed by the immensity before him. "Let me make one thing clear to you. No son of mine is going to sing and prance around a stage like some homo. I didn't fight half a world away so you could waste your life acting like some kind of princess. I do not have a fairy for a son, you got that?"

Unlike the earlier one, this question was rhetorical. James had heard stories from his siblings of what their father was capable of, and while no physical blows were made, the verbal bruising left unique, deep wounds. Being seated in his familiar recliner, he turned the TV back on and, without making eye contact, said, "Go to your room and do homework or something." The discussion was over. It had all the give and take of an NCO dressing down a brand new enlisted man on his first day of boot camp. Sarge had returned.

James stomped toward his bedroom, passing the kitchen and seeing his mother stirring something on the stove. She exchanged a glance with him but offered no help or support in this moment. He secluded himself within his bedroom, lay down on the bed and stared at the ceiling for almost an hour. Most of that time was spent vacillating between rage and regret. Intermittently he thought about what he should do next, yielding no results. He lay in silence with only the distant sound of the local news penetrating his room from the same television he had been exiled from earlier. Enveloped in complete frustration, Jimmy finally made what would become a life-altering decision. He concluded that he was finished. He was finished with everything. There would be no more sports, no more Honor Roll, and no more attempts. James was finished, not just trying to impress his father, but trying altogether. He officially wouldn't care anymore. To him it seemed the only elixir for what he now felt. It hurt too much to live otherwise.

Soon after his private but momentous decision, his mother lightly tapped against his bedroom door. She didn't have to say who it was; he knew his father would never be so subtle. "Come in, Mom," he said.

Claire peeked into his room. James was hoping she would ask about his welfare. Instead, she wondered if he wanted peas or corn for a vegetable at dinner. Rather than answer, James put his hands over his face and started crying. Like his father, he didn't make it a habit of doing so; and in light of his father's recent barrage, he was ashamed at being seen as anything less than Jack's definition of manly. However, the emotion of the moment was just too much.

Closing the door behind her, his mother sat at the foot of his bed and finally asked James how he was doing. "Mom, I've decided I don't care anymore…about anything."

"Oh honey. You really must forgive your father…"

"I don't have to do anything!" James shouted. The declaration was intended to be loud enough for his father to hear but also angry enough for his mother to hear. That would be as much assertiveness as young Jimmy could summon. Lowering his volume, he continued. "I'm not going to do the musical now."

"I know," Claire stated without even a hint of contradicting her husband.

"And I'm not playing football anymore."

"But sweetie, you're so good at it. Your coach thinks you could get a scholarship somewhere when you graduate."

"Don't you get it, Mom? I don't care." James rolled on his side and faced the wall, opposite his mother.

"I just don't want you to make a decision you're going to regret later."

"I don't even care if I regret it," James said defiantly, wiping additional tears from his cheeks.

"How can you say that?" Claire wondered.

James sat up in his bed and looked directly into his mother's eyes. She needed to hear this. "Mom, don't you see? If I don't play, he can't miss my games anymore." He began crying again and placed the heels of his hands on his eyes to somehow stem the tide of emotion that had been unleashed.

Claire never knew what to do at these moments. Not known for her nurturing, she loosely and awkwardly embraced her son, saying nothing. Words always seemed to fail her in conflict. She had made herself the family fire extinguisher, putting out flames wherever she discovered them in the Ramsey home. Unfortunately it did little to assuage the anger and pain experienced by her children. This was only the latest brushfire.

The next day, James had two appointments. First, he turned in his script to the director with his regrets. Secondly, he surprised his coach by telling him that his football career was over. He offered little to no explanation, as none could be given. All he could do was repeatedly apologize for the defensive vacuum his departure would create.

Thus began James Ramsey's journey into mediocrity. Throughout his life, when pressures became too strong or demands became too great, he would look for the proverbial escape hatch. He would emotionally shut down; and now, as a married man and father, he had decided to stop trying yet again. Through his courtship and marriage to Beth, he had shown no opposition to religious things and went with her to church most Sundays. However, after the loss of Christopher, his openness to God had turned on its head and developed into complete ambivalence. Even hatred required some sort of emotion. However, James had none for this God who everyone said was so good but seemed to him like an invisible version of the father he never knew.

Even before Tyler was born, James had determined not to follow in his father's footsteps. He intended that Tyler be whomever he wanted to be without judgment or manipulation. Of course, when his son was young, they had to experiment with many things to see what he gravitated toward and enjoyed.

Tyler was enrolled in soccer when he was four years old. At that age, however, soccer looks more like a moving rugby scrum in which all the players scurry in a huge huddle across the field wherever the ball is. It is not for the purists but makes for many photographable moments. James had played for a few years and enjoyed it before his father's indictment of the sport sent him to baseball. And James had decided he was going to be at every single game Tyler ever played, no matter the cost or inconvenience. He would do whatever he could, short of getting fired, to cheer on his son and encourage him. So he must have been disappointed to see that Tyler did not really enjoy his experience on the field. Within his first couple of games, it became painfully obvious that Tyler had not inherited any of his father's athletic ability. When the ball would roll toward him, he would let loose with a kick and often miss the ball completely. The spectators were kind enough not to laugh at him, but little Tyler seemed to be getting more uncomfortable with each successive game. Privately, on one occasion, James jokingly observed to Beth, "Maybe he'd play better if I didn't show up. That always seemed to help me." He was kidding, but Beth would inevitably chide him for laughing off so much pain in his life.

When that first short season was over, James asked Tyler, "So, do you want to play soccer next time around?" Politely but definitively, Tyler shook his head no. "That's OK, buddy," James said, "We'll find something else for you." James intuitively knew that "something" wasn't going to be sports, and that privately deflated him. Here he was, ready to be the perfect father/coach/spectator that any athlete would want, and now he wouldn't have the chance to cheer him on.

That was reinforced as Tyler's artistic and creative side came to the fore. Even at his young age, it was clear that Tyler took a lot of personal pride in what he drew, colored, or built. Though he couldn't relate to it, James never disparaged it. However, it wasn't long before James began to feel a definable gap between his son and him. This was compounded by the fact that James had no proclivity toward showing affection of any kind. Inwardly, he knew he should. His father's coldness had always frustrated him, but he didn't know how to rectify it. Even embracing his son seemed beyond the scope of his abilities. He privately reasoned that it just wasn't in his personality to do so and hoped his wife could more than make up for the lack. He tried to think of things they could do together as father and son, but most of his attempts missed the mark. He took his son to a professional baseball game, but Tyler seemed more interested in the displays on the outfield scoreboard than what was occurring on the field. He took him to a car show, but his son didn't seem to engage with all the machinery. James saw each attempt as a failure and an indictment on his fatherhood. After a while, just being around

Tyler made him feel like a failure again. What could they enjoy together besides sports?

One thing that always seemed to work for the Ramsey men was being out in nature. There was a city park about a half mile from their home, and sometimes the family would walk there and explore. James initially tried to play catch with Tyler using a Frisbee, but the results only frustrated both of them. Eventually, James discovered that, if he just let Tyler go, he would show him what his interests were. Almost from the time he could walk, Tyler loved to run amidst and around the many trees in the park. For some reason, Tyler would spend extra time around the thick pines that lined the outer boundaries of the park. As became his habit in late summer and early fall, Tyler would search around the pine trees for cones that had fallen from their hosts to the ground below. Each visit was a contest to see how many Tyler could find. His most successful mission yielded eight of them. Each find became a point of celebration for both Ramsey men. James would stay positioned at a picnic table, keeping watch over his son. When Tyler would run back in glee, holding a pine cone, James would yell, "Way to go, Tyler!" It wasn't exactly cheering his boy after a home run, but he would make do.

On each occasion that the men would return home with their plunder, Beth would find a creative way of using them. The first time he brought one home, he and his mother painted it in fall colors; and Tyler gave it to his Sunday School teacher. On another occasion, she hung each pine cone on different doorknobs in the house. When Tyler brought back his haul of eight, she placed them in a bowl, dressed it up with festive ribbon, and created a Christmas centerpiece for the dining room table.

Ten months after Christopher's death, James was spiraling downward. He had detached himself from everything that mattered. Church and religion were far behind him and so was belief in almost anything. Though many years removed, he was still that despondent kid lying on his bed, staring at the ceiling. Once again, a man in his life had taken something from him. Privately, he would become enraged by the belief that he had been duped by religion and all that it promised. He had constantly heard people give testimony to answered prayer. Why not him? Why again was he being passed over, intimidated from hoping for the best? Why must he always be scanning the bleachers for supporters? He had believed in God; why didn't God believe in him?

When those questions remained unanswered, James sought for an alternative solution. He found it in alcohol. About three times a week, he would come home from work carrying nothing but a case of whatever beer was on sale at the liquor store. As he would enter the back door, the case had already been opened and the first can was near completion. A child of alcoholic parents, Beth was highly sensitive to such matters. She permitted a bottle of wine for special occasions, but closely monitored its consumption. The first few times James came home with the case, Beth immediately started interrogating him in the kitchen.

"I asked you to bring home milk. What's that doing here?"

"That's for me," James asserted.

"You expect your son to pour that in his cereal tomorrow?"

James cursed under his breath and responded, "Calm down for once. I'll go back and get some."

"No, I'll take care of it!" Beth said. "The last thing I need to do is send a drunk driver to the store."

"I'm not drunk!"

"At the rate you're going, you'd be three sheets to the wind by the time you came back."

Though a bit dramatic, Beth wasn't far off. She knew the patterns of alcoholics well enough to know that James did not hold his liquor. Two beers and he began slurring words. Three beers and he would tell you what he really thought. Five beers and he became angrier than his father ever was.

"Just get off my back! I've had a hard day…"

"Yeah yeah yeah, and your days are always tougher than anyone else's…"

"Shut up, would ya?" James, still toting the case of beer, marched into the living room where Tyler was in his usual spot, lying on his stomach six feet from the TV screen. Seemingly impervious to his son's presence, he plopped into the large chair, put his feet on the ottoman, placed the case on the end table next to him, picked up the television remote, and switched the channel from the cartoon Tyler was watching to ESPN.

"Hey! I was watching that," Tyler said.

James, opening up his second can, responded, "Don't talk to me that way. I'll watch whatever I want to watch when I'm home. When you start paying the electric bill, you can do the same."

Tyler knew it was a losing battle. He went into the kitchen to help his mother prepare dinner. Beth was always good about finding doable tasks for her son to accomplish. He made it a habit of announcing at the dinner table what he had contributed to the meal, exaggerated or not. "I helped Mom with the mashed potatoes" meant that he had stirred the contents in the pan a few times. "I made the roast" meant that he had turned the oven to 350 degrees. Beth never corrected him. She liked for her son to feel validated.

A half hour later, James, well into his stupor, yelled from his chair in the living room. "Whense dinnr gona be re-ey?"

"About ten minutes," Beth responded.

"Well, it beder be beder than the slop you made lass night."

Perplexed, Tyler looked at his mother for a response, but there was none forthcoming. She simply shook her head and kept her focus on the stove. Tyler wanted to defend her but decided against it.

Dinner that night was quiet. Beth knew her husband had become a powder keg and wanted to protect Tyler from any further damage. Unfortunately, Tyler couldn't help himself. "I made the peas!" he announced.

Not even looking up from his plate, James angrily said, "Tha esplains a lawt!" He pushed his plate with force so that many of the peas previously on its surface now scattered across the table. Tyler immediately began to cry. "Oh, quitsher cryn, you lil…"

"James! Shut up this instant!" Beth shouted, sounding more like a parent than a spouse. "Get away from this table right now!"

Even in his inebriated state, James knew he had crossed the line. He took the rest of the room-temperature beer and retreated to the bedroom. Looking over at her wounded son, she extended her hand toward him. Tyler, with streaks of tears on his cheeks, was hoisted onto his mother's lap, where she embraced her son and kissed him until the intensity of the weeping subsided.

Through the next few weeks, similar scenes played out at the Ramsey house. Beth's only solution was to make dinner and eat with Tyler before James got home. When he arrived, he would be instructed that dinner was waiting in the refrigerator. Tyler found solitude in his room, but it was little comfort. His main goal had become avoiding his father, and it usually worked. Though too young to fully process what was happening to his father, enough harmful things had been said to him to prove he wanted limited contact with him. James seemed more than content not knowing where his son was. Beth had fewer alternatives, however. Most nights, the two of them would argue well into the evening. In bed, Tyler would put the blankets over his head in a vain attempt to block out the battles. After a while, the boy wasn't sure which was worse: his parents arguing when his father was drunk or when he was sober. Without alcohol to diminish his eloquence, James articulated his feelings more keenly and sharply, whereas intoxicated he made little sense but was unpredictable.

On one occasion, Tyler distinctly remembered Beth being blamed for not delivering a healthy baby. In a sober rant, his father used phrases like, "That wouldn't happen on my side of the family," or "Why don't you take better care of yourself?"

"Take care of myself?" Beth responded. "Why don't you look in a mirror sometime and ask that question?"

"And what's that supposed to mean?"

"It means I have a drunk for a husband!"

"I'm not a drunk!"

"Keep saying that, Jim, while you down your hundredth beer this week. Real convincing."

"Well at least I didn't kill a child."

Tyler could hear only silence for about a minute from the vantage point of his bedroom.

Beth was stupefied. "Do you mean to tell me that not only am I responsible for Christopher's death but that I intended for it to happen."

"You took my son away from me!"

"In case you haven't noticed, you have a son that's actually alive and desperately needing his father back."

"Tyler's fine," James snapped.

"He is not fine!"

Even at his young age, it was odd for Tyler to hear two people bantering over his condition as if he weren't just a few feet away.

"All I know," James said, "is that Christopher was going to be the son I hoped and prayed for, and you took him! You just couldn't stand to see me happy, could you?"

Badly injured by his words, Beth went for the jugular. "Well, you have really done it, haven't you? I mean, it took years and years, but you have finally accomplished it. Congratulations, Jim. You've become your father."

Beth's verbal punches landed. James grabbed his coat, wallet, and keys, slamming the back door as he went to the car. Pulling out of the driveway, he sped off to who knows where. In his wake were two people bathed in tears. A wife who no longer recognized her husband and a son who could never be what his father wanted.

As the Christmas season neared, the arguments had largely calmed down but the tension could not have been thicker. Everything had been said that could be said, and unless apologies were forthcoming, a state of détente prevailed. Tyler had become more withdrawn, only speaking when he had to. His only solace was drawing or coloring, which he kept largely contained to his room.

Five days before Thanksgiving, the Ramsey family tried to operate in as normal conditions as possible. Beth headed to the church for a long choir practice in preparation for their Christmas program followed by grocery shopping immediately thereafter. She had long tried to eliminate her husband from the shopping process, as much of his paycheck would inevitably get tied up in alcohol. She would be gone for most of the day. It was a mild Saturday afternoon, and James was watching his beloved Ohio State Buckeyes play a crucial Big Ten conference game on television. He was accompanied by his ever-present can of beer. With a noon kickoff, James was well on his way to a drunken haze by halftime. Tyler stayed in his room, drawing pictures on an art pad his mother had purchased for him.

"Tyler! Gitscher butt in here!" James barked.

Obediently but nervously, Tyler stopped what he was doing and walked into the living room. As if sensing his presence behind his beloved chair, James said, "Why don-choo make yu-self yoofful and git-cher dad a beer?" Tyler couldn't help but notice that his dad didn't even make eye contact with him in delivering the request. Retrieving a can from the refrigerator, Tyler stopped next to his dad's chair and held it up for him. Angrily snatching it from his hand, James quickly focused again on the football game. Tyler, not waiting for an acknowledgment, returned to his room.

The unfortunate thing for Tyler that day was that Ohio State was losing. With apparently few things to live for, James had put what was left of his emotional hopes and dreams on a group of college students from Columbus. By their lackluster performance that afternoon, it seemed the Scarlet and Grey didn't understand how important this was to him. As the fourth quarter further cemented the fact that the Buckeyes were about to suffer their first loss, Tyler could hear his father spout all kinds of unintelligible profanities. Trying to block out the horrid noise, he concentrated on his Legos as he tried to construct a neighborhood of his own creation.

"Tyler!" James angrily snarled.

Assuming he was being called upon for another beer run, the boy stopped near his father's chair and waited for orders. But he was surprised to hear his dad say, "Lissen. I haff an idea. Wussay we go to the park and gessome...and gessome pine cones."

Tyler's face lit up at the possibility. It would be the first father-son activity he would undertake in months. He couldn't contain his enthusiasm, jumping up and down and shouting, "Yes! Yes! Yes!"

James continued, "Heerse wha I wan choo to do. Putsher coat on and head over. Yoos start lucking and I'll be by soon."

Tyler didn't need to hear it twice. Putting on his shoes and donning a thick jacket, he ran out the front door and didn't slow down until he arrived at the park so filled with glorious memories. Like a bird freed from its cage, he ran with abandon around the pine trees as he had done the previous few years. It wasn't long before he found his quarry. Within minutes he had discovered at least five of them. But what to do? It would have been easy to collect all of them and put them on the nearby picnic table in anticipation of his father's arrival. However, that wasn't the payoff he was looking for. There was nothing better in his life than hearing that, "Way to go, Tyler!" he got every year at this time. Nothing was going to spoil that for him. Initially running the circumference of the park to scout all the fallen cones, he now went back and walked the same route, paying careful attention to any that had eluded his gaze before.

As he rounded every tree, he would go back into the open and look at the picnic table, checking on his father's imminent arrival. Finding it empty, he would return to his search. After his second round of inspection, he came back to the picnic table and decided to wait. He waited for a while, it seemed. Eventually he would wander from the picnic table and look in the distance at the path that led to his house to see if his father was on the way. He wasn't. To pass the time, the young adventurer decided to do a third round of exploring the same terrain. Each time, however, yielded no more finds than his previous journeys.

Not wanting to waste the moment he longed for, Tyler sat at the picnic table, watched, and waited.

With a trunk full of grocery bags, Beth pulled into the Ramsey driveway. Opening the back door, she said, "Hey there! Need some help!" She headed back to the car and grabbed two bags. As she headed to the back door again, she noticed that no one had come to her aid. Walking back into the house and placing the bags on the kitchen counter, she once again announced her arrival. She could hear the TV but nothing else. "Jim? Tyler?" Leaving the back door open, she walked into the living room and saw her spouse sprawled out on the stuffed chair. "Tyler!" Beth yelled in desperation. Jogging to his room, she opened the door and found it empty. She sprinted back to the living room and began violently shaking her intoxicated husband. "Wake up! Wake up!"

A cursory inspection of the end table revealed that at least 10 beers had been consumed by her husband since she had left for the church. James showed signs of life, but was nowhere near being aware of his surroundings. "Jim, where is our son?"

James could hardly even make auditory sounds. He was barely conscious. He wrinkled his face in response to her question, as if he had no idea what had become of their eldest child. Beth now became aggressive, slapping James in the face and shaking him once again to briefly awake him from his overwhelming stupor.

"You listen to me and listen good. I'm going to find our son, and when I get back you had better not be here. In fact, I don't want you here anymore. I don't care where you go, where you sleep, or what you do as long as it isn't here, do you understand? Do you understand?" James nodded and Beth returned him to his previous position on the chair. "I mean it! You leave right now. If you're here when I get back, I'm calling the police. I don't ever want to see you here again."

Returning to the kitchen, she noticed that Tyler's shoes and jacket were missing, so he must have voluntarily gone somewhere. Closing the trunk lid with most of the groceries she purchased still inside, she started the car and began driving around the neighborhood in a desperate search for her son.

Twilight was quickly giving way to darkness, so time was of the essence. Maybe Tyler had gone to Violet Birnbaum's house looking for refuge. She stopped at her home, but Violet had not seen or heard from Tyler. Returning to her car and scouring the neighborhood, Beth became frantic, pleading aloud to God to help her find her little boy. Tyler wasn't one to roam into unfamiliar territory, so she stayed within a few blocks of their home, driving in circles, hoping to catch a glimpse of him in her headlights.

After about three passes around the immediate neighborhood, she came near the park and decided to investigate within. She would need to park the car and go by foot from there. It had been a while since she had been here and never in the dark. Beth was careful not to collide with unseen obstacles. She continually yelled out Tyler's name, listening for anything that sounded more like human over animal life.

Ten minutes into her search, she passed through some large pine trees into a clearing. It was then that she heard something. Whatever it was, it was muffled. She moved in the direction of the faint voice, shouting his name. In the early evening light, she could barely make out a picnic table and a small person sitting at it with his feet not nearly reaching the ground. His forehead was pressed against his arms on the table's surface, and the muffled sound she had heard moments before were now more readily identifiable as sobbing.

Instantly relieved, Beth wanted to pick up her son in her arms and squeeze him tight, but there was clearly another issue to deal with here. Sitting next to him at the picnic table and putting her arm around Tyler's small shoulders, she waited to see what her son would do next.

Lifting his head slightly and looking forward into space, Tyler said, "Where's Dad? Why didn't Dad come?" With the left sleeve of his jacket, he wiped away the latest coating of what had clearly been many tears shed. Beth instantly connected the dots. "Dad said he was coming. Where is he?" Beth found herself in the least admired position possible. She had to quickly decide what her son needed to hear. Would she shade the truth and make excuses for a man who had clearly neglected his parental duties? Would she tell him the harsh reality that his father may have chosen booze over his son and put him in a dangerous position? "Tyler, I can't defend your father. He's been a mess, and he's doing stupid things. What he did today was wrong, so I told him he needs to leave the house for a while until he gets better."

Beth hoped it would be welcoming news to Tyler, but it was nothing of the sort. He was jolted by the news and wondered if the whole thing was his fault. He didn't like his father the way he was, but he didn't want him to leave either. Tyler started crying again. Beth embraced him for a while, occasionally patting his back with her hand. They remained at the picnic table for a while. Though the decreasing temperatures made it uncomfortable to remain, Beth wanted to make sure her husband was gone by the time they returned to the house.

When the intensity of emotion eventually lifted, Beth asked, "Tyler, do you still want to get a pine cone for me? I'd hate to go home empty handed. Is there one close by? Beth couldn't really see it, but Tyler nodded. He got up from the table and walked about 20 yards to the well-scouted cone he had found hours earlier. Within a minute, he had returned with it and placed it on the table for his mother.

"What are you going to do with it?" Tyler wondered.

"Not sure yet," Beth answered, "but I'll figure out something. Come on. Let's go."

Beth got up from the picnic table and lifted Tyler to a standing position. Holding the pine cone with one hand and grasping Tyler's hand with the other, she carefully led him toward the parking lot and the waiting car. Not another word was exchanged that evening, Tyler was going to bed immediately after arriving home. It would also be the last time Tyler and his mother would discuss that fateful day. He never had the courage to bring it up, and Beth never seemed in the right frame of mind to revisit those painful memories.

Though his parents would divorce soon after the incident and Tyler would initially see his father monthly, it did little to appease the doubt and anger he would feel about that day. His contact with his father became diminished after James remarried. Tyler never knew whether it was his father's choice to do so, or an attempt to curry favor with his new wife. By the time he was in high school, his contact with his father would be limited to a birthday card in the spring and a Christmas present mailed to the house.

He never said it aloud, but Tyler continually wondered what he could have done differently that day that would have changed the outcome. Maybe he could have been more attentive to his dad's needs. He probably should have gone back home from the park after a while so that his mother wouldn't have been the wiser. Maybe if he could have been what his father hoped for, none of this would ever have happened. No matter how he replayed the events of that Saturday in his mind, the result was always the same: It was his fault. No one ever made such a claim, but no one needed to. He knew the truth.

A few days after the incident, on tree-trimming day, Beth had a surprise for Tyler. She wanted to do something extra special to improve his mood during this first Christmas without his father. While Tyler was setting out all the ornaments for the tree, his mother disappeared into the kitchen and returned with her hands behind her back.

Tyler, instantly knowing something was up, asked, "What are you hiding, Mom?"

"Well, I came up with something."

Perplexed by his mother's reply, Tyler could only say, "Huh?"

Beth brought her hands forward. Cradled in them was the pine cone from that horrible day in the park. It had been rolled in glitter, spray-painted green, and fastened to a loop of red ribbon. "I decided to make something that we could hang onto permanently from all your pine cone quests."

Tyler received the craft half-heartedly. His lack of response hurt Beth, as she was hoping for a better reaction. Later that night, she thought it was probably too much to ask that an ornament could somehow undo all the damage of that day, not to mention the months previous to it. However, Tyler said nothing negative and was glad to add it to the ensemble of decorations.

When the tree was finished later that night, Beth continued their tradition of plugging in the finished tree and sitting with her son on the couch to admire their handiwork. As instrumental Christmas music played in the background, both artists silently stared at their creation with obvious thoughts in their head. Finally, it would be young Tyler who would say what was on both their minds. "I wish we were all together."

"I wish we were all together," Pastor Wilkins uttered, having finished his explanation of the three gifts of the Magi. "I know that probably sounds odd to say, because clearly God doesn't feel or react to things in a human manner. However, we are created in His image. So, if you'll permit me, I want to take an angle on the Christmas story you may not have heard before."

Tyler now back in the present and filled to the brim with emotion, sat up straight in his pew while trying to retain some semblance of composure.

"Remember that it wasn't only the Wise Men who were far from home, for on that Christmas night, our Savior, the Son of God, made the greatest journey in the history of mankind. Our Lord left His place in heaven, willingly leaving that wonderful place of worship and glory, and placing Himself on the field of battle. He was far from home, in a sense. Though the Father was always with Him, it wasn't the same. He had made the trip from perfection to imperfection, from security to insecurity.

"Not only that, but He made the indefinable journey of being God in all ways to being man in addition. He had gone from the throne room of heaven to the womb of a teenage girl. How can anyone accurately describe it? Could anyone be further from the Father He knew and loved?

"You see, Jesus understands loneliness. He knows what it's like to be away from people you dearly love. And if you feel that way this Christmas Eve night, He is here to remind you that you're not alone."

This was usually the point at which Tyler would excuse himself from his near-back-row seat and head for home, rationalizing that it had been enough. However, now he was front-and-center with people on either side of him and on Christmas Eve at that. To even use the restroom now would be a major distraction from the service. He felt the emotional walls closing in on him, and he desperately wanted to flee. Like a frightened child on a roller coaster, he lowered his chin to his chest and closed his eyes trying to ride it out.

Pastor Wilkins continued. "I know that most Christmas Eve services are more ceremonial in nature, but tonight I want to depart from that. This evening, I want to give you an opportunity to come and receive prayer. Maybe you have never made a life commitment to Jesus. If so, this is your night. Come and receive. However, I know that there must be those tonight who already know the Lord but are feeling so far from home in one way or another. I don't want you facing tomorrow or any more tomorrows feeling that way again. I would like for our elders and their spouses to come to the front. They are ready to receive you and minister to you tonight. Won't you come?"

As the congregation stood and the chorus of "O Come All Ye Faithful" began to play, Tyler could not escape the fact that he needed to respond to this message. It had been so long since he had prayed by himself, let alone in front of hundreds of people. He was only about 30 feet away from the elders, but it seemed to be dozens of miles. Truth be known, he didn't even know what he would say when he got up there. He knew only that he needed to move forward.

Placing his hand on Dave Kirschner's back, he whispered "Excuse me" and shuffled his way past a handful of people and stepped into the aisle. Not knowing any of the people up front, he made a straight line and hoped the couple he drifted toward wouldn't be freaked out by him. He looked at the carpet as he walked forward, already feeling ashamed for having to do this. He felt all eyes on him, though he certainly wasn't the only one taking advantage of this opportunity.

Mere steps away from the platform, the waters of people parted before him; and, when he looked up, he saw a familiar man wearing a black suit, red tie, and white kerchief.

Pastor Wilkins placed his hands on Tyler's shoulders and brought him closer. "Tyler..."

He wondered how he knew his name. He had never spoken to the pastor before and definitely had never stayed after church long enough to even shake his hand.

"Tyler, I know this sounds strange, but I have been waiting for this opportunity."

Tyler had been afraid of getting someone out of sorts. Now he was the one freaking out.

"Do you believe God brings people together?"

Tyler believed that until 24 hours ago when a certain young lady prematurely ended his most meaningful relationship. Now he wasn't so sure.

"For months, God has put you on my heart. I would be preaching and see you in the back, but I never got the chance to meet you. So I started praying for you, not even knowing what you were going through. One week, I noticed you talking to the Bennetts, so I asked them to tell me what they could. I hope that's OK."

Tyler nodded, eyes still affixed to the carpet. Roger, wanting to make sure the young man grasped every word, took his right hand off Tyler's shoulder and placed it on the side of his face. Reflexively, Tyler lifted his gaze so that the two men were eye-to-eye.

"Tyler, I can't imagine how hard all this must be, your first Christmas without your mother." Tyler closed his eyes briefly again, unsure of what to do. "But I really want you to hear this tonight." Tyler regained his line of sight, looking into the face of this man he had admired from afar. "God isn't finished with you; don't be finished with Him." Wilkins then stepped forward and leaned into Tyler's ear, praying so that he alone could hear it. At some point during that prayer, Tyler stopped listening, not because he was averse to what was being said, but because his emotions could no longer be contained. For the first time in years, tears flowed freely. His mind raced with memories of wounds sustained – the breakup last night, his mother's death, his father's departure – it seemed to mesh together into one glorious outburst. Instinctively, he leaned forward so that his face was pressed against Roger's suit jacket. He would later offer to pay for the dry cleaning bill for the jacket, but his pastor would laugh it off, remarking that they were treasured battle scars he didn't want to soon forget.

When the prayer was finished, Pastor Wilkins embraced this young man he had now barely met. Tyler wasn't offended by the gesture in the least, but it was a new experience for him. He wasn't sure if he had ever shared a moment like that with a man in all his life. Something about it felt very right. He immediately thought it was something that had been grossly missing but needed to be experienced again. Inwardly, he compared it to the first time he had tried a favorite food.

Releasing the embrace, Pastor Wilkins said, "Stay right here, OK?" Tyler remained in place. Only then did he look around and realize that most of the people were already gone. No doubt many had plans, and how long had he been up there anyway? Rather than do his usual thorough dissection of events, he cleared his mind and waited for Roger to return.

"I want you to have this, Tyler. I know with technology being what it is that a printed Bible seems antiquated, but I want you to have this as a gift from the church and a remembrance of this evening."

This was the first Bible he had received as a gift since his treasured childhood experience of winning the contest at his Vacation Bible School so many years before. He also realized this may be the only gift he would receive this Christmas.

"Thank you so much. I will treasure it always." Tyler meant every word of it. He hoped he would never forget that service and the chance to connect with his pastor and, more importantly, with the Lord again. Turning around, he noticed Wally and Jackie standing in the aisle waiting for him. Jackie stretched her hands forward to receive the young man, pulled him in and kissed him on the cheek.

"We love you, Tyler!" Jackie said, wiping tears from her eyes. Tyler could only smile as he looked at this precious couple who had done so much for him.

Wally broke the tension. "You should know that it takes someone special to ruin my wife's makeup like that." He exhaled in laughter as his wife playfully slapped him on the shoulder.

"Oh, I must look absolutely ghastly," Jackie responded, blotting her eyes with a tissue from her purse.

Quick to repair the damage, Wally kissed his wife's forehead and said, "You look just fine."

The Kirschners were waiting in the lobby talking to a handful of people who had stuck around for conversation. Now joined by the trio from the sanctuary, Wally said, "Well, why don't we go back to the house?"

Tyler said, "You know, I think I'm just going to walk home from here."

"Oh, sweetie! Are you sure?" Sue asked, now feeling as if she had a vested interest in the young man.

"Yeah, I'm pretty tired. Besides, I feel great. I think I might head home and do some painting before turning in."

"Well, all right. If you say so," Wally retorted. "But we don't want you spending Christmas alone, so I'll call you in the morning and we'll plan something OK?"

Knowing their difference in body clocks, Tyler said, "How 'bout noon?"

Both older couples erupted in laughter, always entertained by the sleeping habits of the young. They exchanged handshakes and hugs, and Tyler began the eight-block walk home to the loft. The evening was crisp with temperatures in the low 30s, but there was no wind off the lake which made the walk much more tolerable. As he traversed through mostly quiet streets and blinking traffic lights, Tyler thought about what Pastor Wilkins had said to him at the front. Pondering each word, Tyler reasoned that he was nowhere near finished with God, though he had been acting like it. He began whispering a prayer to the Lord, sorry for his long silence, asserting he would do better in the future.

Still, he couldn't help wondering what Pastor had meant by the fact that God wasn't finished with him.

Ten

Unlocking the door and entering his apartment, Tyler turned on the light that lit his entryway. Sauntering into the living room, he switched on a couple of lamps, removed his jacket, untucked his shirt and flopped onto the sofa. Once seated, he placed the new Bible he had received on the cushion next to him. As he quietly reflected on the evening's events, he had to wonder what left him more exhausted: the pain from yesterday's breakup or this unplanned excursion down memory lane.

To his right was the unlit Christmas tree that only 24 hours before was a figment of his imagination. To his left lay his studio and the unfinished canvas that seemed to beg for his attention. He wondered if what he had experienced in the previous hour had empowered him to paint or rid him of all creative energy. Of course, artists face the same choice daily. Rare are the days when one is inspired to create; rather, it is an act of volition pure and simple no different from the guy who rolls out of bed at 5:00 in the morning to run a few miles.

In a sense, Tyler had been roused from his slumber. A spiritual and emotional morning had dawned, and he knew he had to capitalize upon it. Hoping for one last source of inspiration, he decided to replicate an annual moment from his childhood. Rising from the sofa, he darkened the lamps he had switched on minutes before. Now in complete darkness, he groped his way through familiar surroundings with only the glow of city lights through his studio windows to illuminate him. Kneeling down at the Christmas tree, he reached behind it on the carpet until he felt the plug that connected all the strings of light on the tree. Hoping not to mildly electrocute himself, he carefully probed his hands along the wall until he felt an outlet plate. It took a few attempts, but eventually he was able to fit the plug into the outlet.

This was the first time he was able to behold his creation in the dark of night, just as he had done with his mother many times before. He returned to the sofa and gazed upon the new Ramsey tree with all its imperfections. It was a good first solo effort, especially considering the circumstances under which it was put together. It seemed emotionally hollow to behold a Christmas tree as he was without his mother being there too. The absence of Beth and the painful sense of loss that accompanied it were now inescapable. It seemed everything he had gained in the church service was in danger of ebbing away with this new threat.

Tyler stood and walked to his studio, turning on the lamp that brightened his work space. Looking again upon the canvas, he saw the undecorated tree just waiting for acrylic tinsel, lights, and ornaments to be added. No imagination necessary. It was all before him.

He decided to paint the way he had decorated, one adornment at a time: first the lights, then the tinsel, and lastly the ornaments. Painting such intricate detail was painstaking work, but Tyler felt an obligation to his craft and his own honor to do exquisite work. After the tinsel was finished, Tyler made a pot of coffee to give himself the necessary fuel to finish the project before dawn, Christmas day. Painting the lights was slow going, having to do so many of them in so many different colors. Halfway through, he was tempted to make them all white and be done with it, but he stuck with it for the sake of authenticity.

At brief moments, a random thought of, "What are you going to do with this thing?" would run through his mind.

Avoiding the temptation to analyze, he concluded as before that this work was for him so it didn't matter. Who cared if he ever sold it? This, he believed, is where he went wrong as an artist. Somewhere along the line, he had stopped painting to please himself but continually thought of potential commercial appeal in his work. He felt he had bowed at the altar of financial survival rather than personal satisfaction. If God looked upon His creation and said it was good, shouldn't he be able to do the same?

Clearing this mental hurdle gave the budding artist new life. He painted the twine ornaments with all their flaws, then set about recreating the specialized and handmade ornaments, some of which he had revisited hours before. Each one elicited acute emotional reactions. Now he was allowing himself to feel the impact of each moment, good or bad. Frequently, he would pause to look out the windows upon the quiet city, meditating on the events of his life and how his mother had tried to soften the blow or increase the joy of each moment.

Only now did he begin to appreciate all she was and all she had tried to do. He wasn't sure what he would have done in her position. At times, it had been easy to judge, privately wondering what drew her to his father, why she stayed with him as long as she did, and why she couldn't talk about the deepest hurts of their lives. Now he decided it was time to put down his gavel. She wasn't a perfect lady, but he was fortunate to have had her in his life. More than anything, he was thankful she had always been there for him.

Like the tree, he saved the Bible ornament for last. He imagined his mother's face each time she affixed it to the tree. There was something about it that illumined her expression. It was her chief inspiration through the wins and losses of her life, even at the end.

"Yeah, the end," Tyler said aloud. Putting his brush in a jar of water and laying aside his palette, he looked at what seemed to be the completion of his quest. It pleased him, but the feeling of accomplishment was quickly set aside for the memories that had just been stirred. Returning to the sofa, he laid his head back and closed his eyes. The glow from the tree was still lighting the room, but Tyler suddenly wasn't interested in that. He was exhausted but not sleepy. Regretting the coffee he had drunk, he wondered if he would be completely robbed of sleep this night.

Opening his eyes again, he looked next to him at the surprise gift he had received from Pastor Wilkins. It had been a long time since he had cracked open a Bible. The guilt of it almost kept him from even grasping it in his hand. Ah, the guilt! Tyler couldn't remember a time when it wasn't his constant companion. It seemed Tyler Ramsey was the most responsible person in the world, for no matter what went wrong, Tyler held himself responsible. In the absence of explanation or understanding, it seemed the easiest and best solution. However, Tyler failed to realize the toll this pattern of thinking had taken on him.

He thought again of the church service and the sense of a fresh start it brought. Refusing to dwell upon what he hadn't been doing, he decided to just do the right thing now. Taking the new Bible in hand, he leaned back and took a closer look. It had a faux-leather cover, which made sense, as the real thing would be quite the expense for any church. It was visually appealing and had the same gold-edged pages that his mother's Bible had. He didn't have a specific target in mind of what or where to read, so he decided to start in Matthew 2, the same passage Pastor Wilkins had used in his message earlier.

Tyler loved the feel of a new book. He loved opening it wide for the first time and hearing the distinct crack the spine would make to allow the reader access. Nicer Bibles would easily lie flat, except for passages in Genesis or Revelation, but Tyler's new Bible was more tightly bound and would need to be held with both hands at all times. In spite of its lack of frills, the Bible was a welcome new addition for Tyler.

He opened it in the middle and came upon the latter half of Psalms. Holding it open with his hands, he used his right thumb to glide across the edges of the pages. There was something about the feel of a Bible. Sometimes he would take Beth's beloved King James and leaf through it a page at a time. He would search for notes that she had written in the margins, sermon outlines from years gone by that were scrawled in blank spaces, or verses that had been underlined. He slowed his scriptural search to a crawl, fully appreciating the texture of each page sliding against his skin as he continued past Proverbs then the prophetical books on his way to the New Testament.

Only then did he remember another Bible.

Beth had first been diagnosed when Tyler was still in high school, a few months from graduation. She had detected a lump on her breast, and her doctor had immediately ordered her to undergo a lumpectomy to test for cancer. All this had occurred without her son's knowledge. Beth figured that if it had been benign, there was no sense of putting him through the worry. That was always Beth's nature, going through about ten times as much as she let on. She always felt uncomfortable being fussed over. While some church members request prayer every time they get the sniffles, Beth was the type who would go under the knife without letting her pastor know. She never demanded or even expected visits at the hospital and didn't want to be the focus of great attention.

Of course, when Tyler found out the news that his mother had breast cancer, he was initially angry – at God for allowing it and at his mother for not letting him know sooner. "From here on out," he announced, "I am going to be part of everything; every test, procedure, surgery, and treatment. Do you understand?" It was the only time Tyler would turn the tables on her and act parental. She got the message. From that point on, Tyler would be her personal companion and chauffeur for most of her medical treatments. Initially insisting that she could drive herself to and from her chemotherapy appointments, Beth changed her mind when she became immediately nauseous from the treatments. She was a tough lady, but the potency from the dosage she was receiving could take down a giant.

Displaying a tough exterior, it was still difficult for Tyler to keep his coolheadedness at times. More than once on his way back to the suburbs with Beth in the passenger seat, he would have to pull off the interstate so his mother could open her door, kneel on the shoulder of the road, and vomit on the concrete. It was the most helpless Tyler would ever feel and an image he would never entirely forget.

When he wasn't driving Beth to the hospital for treatments, Tyler was stopping by the house almost daily to check on her. She continued to work, as she needed the paycheck to help with the expenses of the house. He would come by in the evenings and make her dinner as often as possible. He would stay for a couple of hours before heading back to the dorm, usually at Beth's insistence. "Tyler, I'm all right. You don't have to be my nurse-maid. I am perfectly capable of caring for myself. You have studying to do." It was normally some form of these lines that signaled to Tyler that it was time to go back to campus. Beth could not tolerate putting people out, and she privately thought she was stealing time from her son when he should be enjoying college life. While Tyler always tried not to overstay, he would not hear of Beth going through the trials of cancer alone.

Shortly after her diagnosis, Beth underwent a double mastectomy. Tyler felt so limited in his ability to provide emotional help for such losses. There were obvious chronological and gender differences that prevented him from doing so. Outside of her son and a few dysfunctional relatives, Beth had no family support system. He encouraged her to join a support group, but he was almost immediately laughed off. "Oh please!" Beth said, "If there's one thing we don't need more of, it's people whining and complaining about their problems to the whole world." Even though Tyler was taking an introductory Psychology class in college, he had to wonder if her apparent stubbornness was due to the way her generation dealt with adversity or because she was the daughter of alcoholic parents. He definitely couldn't ask her, that was for sure.

One of the bright spots in Beth's life was her new church. She had settled at Calvary Fellowship for a number of reasons. It was only a couple of miles from the Ramsey house, embraced her style of worship and, with a congregation of around 500, provided Beth with the anonymity she wanted. Tyler was impressed with the determination the church showed in making her part of the community. Initially resistant, Beth eventually decided to join one of the church's many small groups. When she felt up to it, she would drive to the meeting house on Friday nights, but once she made known her medical challenges to the home group, others would pick her up if she didn't feel up to driving. Tyler was relieved; not only was his mother opening herself once again to others but he wasn't the only one shouldering the emotional load.

The oddest part of the "cancer journey," as his mother would sometimes call it, was that mother and son never really talked about it. Neither seemed to know whether or how to broach the subject. Beth thought that talking about her pain and treatments would only incur greater stress on her son. Tyler thought that the last thing his mother wanted to talk about was cancer. She lived with it 24 hours a day. Surely she needed a reprieve from all that. They were like two nations negotiating peace but neither willing to be the first to make concessions. It was further proof that at the heart of many of life's disappointments is false assumption.

Conversations would usually revolve around Tyler's studies or Beth's church. Of course, this discourse of talking without really talking was quite normal in the Ramsey household. However, as Tyler moved from his home to the dormitory and began to take undergrad courses, he began to ask himself big questions about his formative years. Sometimes he would go see his mom for the express purpose of confronting her about their rough historical family issues; but something about the conversation and his nerve would convince him otherwise every time. His mother's illness seemed to take up so much emotional space that he felt it wrong to also bring up the past.

Cancer is that rarest of diseases in which the treatment seems much more brutal than the sickness. Tyler supposed it was necessary, but chemotherapy seemed the most barbaric thing ever proposed by man. The side effects – hair loss, vomiting, constant fatigue – seemed so horrific that it was difficult to find anyone who could enumerate its actual benefits. That, combined with his mother's double mastectomy, tore away at her treasured femininity. Her beauty was a large part of her identity, so she did what she could to compensate. For weeks she discriminately searched for just the right wig to most closely resemble her familiar quaff. "I'm not putting some raccoon on my head," she would stubbornly say. "I'm not Davy Crockett!"

Often after a treatment, Tyler would get her home, have her lie on the couch, put a blanket on her, make sure she had everything she needed within arm's reach, and leave her be. She would frequently fall asleep and remain there through the night. How she was able to still work was beyond explanation, but necessity often brings about the superhuman in all of us.

After a round of chemotherapy followed by another round of radiation treatments, Beth was tested and proclaimed to be in remission. Beth said she was healed, and her church family celebrated. Tyler was more cautious. Life had taught him not to get very excited about anything, as it could change at a moment's notice. Beth often confronted Tyler about his latent cynicism, to which Tyler jokingly responded that it made him a better artist. During her remission, Beth came into her own. Her brush with mortality seemed to free her to take greater risks and try new things. She went on excursions with women in her church, going to religious conferences or taking trips to Amish country and Myrtle Beach. Though it was a huge departure from the woman he grew up with, Tyler took solace in the fact that his mother's life seemed to be more carefree and happier than ever.

The happiness would be short-lived. Soon after Tyler moved into the loft downtown, the cancer returned. Beth was devastated; Tyler was unfortunately unsurprised. Whatever the doctor told her, Tyler would never know. She would say only that the cancer had returned, but that was all. She reverted to her "need to know only" basis with her son and, judging by the lack of information given to him, she didn't think he needed to know much. In mid-November, while they were having dinner at a Mexican restaurant, Beth announced, "I need you to take me to St. Luke's Hospital next week. Is that OK?'

"Sure, mom. Is it for a treatment?"

"No. It looks like they want me to stay for a few days so they can run a few tests." Beth was so matter-of-fact, one would have thought she was talking about getting an oil change for her Buick.

"Is it serious?"

"I don't think so. They just want to poke and prod me as much as possible, I guess."

"Do they want to see if the cancer has spread?" Tyler wondered.

Beth was impatient and raised her voice. "I don't know, Tyler!" The tables and booths nearest them put down their collective forks and looked in their direction. Realizing her brief disturbance, Beth lowered her voice and leaned forward. "Look, I just need a ride to the hospital next Wednesday. Can you do it or not?"

Tyler retreated. "OK, OK, I can do it. Sorry."

And that ended their last great cancer "discussion." The next Wednesday, Tyler dutifully picked up Beth from the house, suitcase and shoulder bag in tow, and took her to the hospital. Initially demanding that Tyler drop her off and leave, Beth could not convince him to do so. He accompanied her through the admitting process, including following her to her room on the fifth floor. Upon arrival, Tyler put down both bags.

"All right. I guess I'll take it from here," Beth said.

"OK, Mom. You need anything else?"

"Nope. I'm all set."

Tyler didn't know what to do next, so he hugged his mother and wished her well. He promised to be back the next day.

Beth wouldn't hear of it. "I'll be fine. If I'm still here during the weekend, swing on by if you get a chance." Tyler agreed and was on his way.

When he returned to the loft, he made a point of calling Calvary Fellowship to make sure they were aware of Beth's hospitalization. Unsurprisingly, they didn't know. He also asked if someone could contact the leader of her home group to make them aware. By the time he returned to St. Luke's on Saturday, her room was filled with various flower and balloon bouquets. A couple from the church was praying with her as he walked through the door. Beth had a clearly positive disposition. As usual, she had taken great pains to put on makeup for the occasion. It seemed she was always ready for her close-up.

After saying "Amen," Beth introduced the well-dressed couple to her son. "Oh, it's great to finally meet you," said the husband who looked more like a catalog model than a church member. "Your mother brags about you all the time."

Expectedly, Tyler blushed and looked down at the tile floor. Quickly brushing the praise aside without acknowledging the compliment, he said, "Thank you both for coming to visit my mom. I know it means a lot to her."

The even-more-beautiful wife chimed in, "Well, she means a lot to us, too."

After a few seconds of silence, they reached what Tyler would sometimes call the Pentecostal Pregnant Pause. In other words, that precise moment (usually occurring in a lobby after a church service) when people had absolutely nothing left to say but could only smile at one another. Fortunately for them, Tyler was an expert at breaking tension. "Well," he said, "thanks again for coming by. Feel free to drop by anytime." They all shook hands, and the couple exited the room. Moving bedside, Tyler surveyed the room and was overwhelmed by the amount of trinkets that had been purchased for her. "Wow! You made out like a bandit."

"Oh yeah. And it only took getting cancer for the second time." Beth smiled wryly, a rare unveiling of her sometimes dark sense of humor that Tyler had inherited.

"Mom, you are so bad. Do your church friends ever get exposed to this material?"

"No, I save that for you," she again replied sarcastically.

For Tyler, it was a good sign. "You look good, Mom. Are they going to let you out of here for Thanksgiving?"

"Eh, I'm not sure. They might keep me here a little longer than that."

The news came as a surprise to Tyler, who mentally was already making Christmas decorating plans. He tried to ask a few follow-up questions, but Beth was not forthcoming, brushing aside each one in her usual matter-of-fact manner.

Tyler quickly relented and spent the rest of his visit bringing his mother up to date on his artwork and his job at the steakhouse.

"Sweetie, why don't you use your degree to land a job teaching art somewhere?" Tyler anticipated this question, as it would make its presence known regularly after his graduation. And like his queries about his mother's health, he would brush these aside with a canned response, "Mom, schools aren't going anywhere. They'll be there if I need them. This is my one chance to do what I love. I have to at least try." Beth would shake her head in befuddlement and end it at that.

Thanksgiving for the Ramseys took place on the fifth floor of St. Luke's Hospital. Beth's prediction was correct, as she remained a patient. Initially insisting that he spend it with his aunt and uncle or one of his church families, Beth reluctantly agreed for Tyler to spend the day with her. He did his best to make the day like normal. He arrived just before 9 a.m. so they could watch the Macy's Thanksgiving Day Parade together in her room. Tyler was always good at providing commentary on the event, taking issue with celebrities' wardrobe choices and their sometimes inability to properly lip sync to their own songs while on the float.

As jaded as Tyler could be, the kid in him would come out when the gigantic balloons would make their appearance. Beth always loved the bands and each year would wonder why Tyler had never participated in the band in high school. "Mom, I got made fun of enough," he would usually respond.

Though they spent an enjoyable holiday together, Tyler could at times tell that Beth wasn't herself. He would allude to Thanksgivings past and to different family dinners and activities. Beth would remain silent, to which Tyler would ask, "You remember that, Mom?" Beth would look toward the ceiling, no doubt in an effort to recall the information. Rather than say she couldn't, she would just look again at the television screen and hope Tyler would change the subject.

Tyler chalked it up to the treatment she was receiving, though he didn't know the specifics of what it was. It clearly wasn't chemo, as his mother retained the hair she grew back after her previous experience with it. Occasional questions to her doctors the previous weeks were usually met with an insistence on getting the information from his mother instead. Tyler knew that was a fruitless pursuit and assumed that no news was good news.

Thanksgiving dinner that day consisted of a turkey/ mashed potatoes special from the hospital cafeteria. Beth had a tray of soup broth, jello, and applesauce brought to her. "Just like the Pilgrims ate," Beth jokingly noted. She was clearly exhausted by mid-afternoon and fell asleep while they watched an old movie in her room. Tyler decided to take his leave. Gathering his coat, he bent down, kissed his mother on the forehead and headed home. Tyler hoped it would be the last Thanksgiving they would spend together like that. He was more right than he realized.

Over the next couple of weeks, Beth's health deteriorated. By early December, she had stopped fixing herself up for potential visitors, as she rarely had the energy to sit up in bed. In addition, it was difficult to engage her in conversation as she largely kept her eyes shut. Tyler wasn't sure if it was from the fatigue, pain-killing drugs or the lack thereof. Tyler was seeing her every day, and each visit seemed to reveal one more layer peeled away from the mystique that was his mother.

The visits became difficult soon after. To him, it was one thing to see her deplete physically but quite another when she began losing her mental faculties. Elizabeth Ramsey wasn't a perfect person, but her mind was quicker than any other person's Tyler had ever known. Two weeks after Thanksgiving, he came by one afternoon to see her. The attending nurse stopped him in the hallway and asked him to wait before going into the room. He figured they were doing something of a private nature, so he thought nothing of it and waited near the nurse's station. When her doctor approached, Tyler politely exchanged pleasantries but was surprised when he engaged him in conversation.

"Tyler, do you have a moment?"

"Sure. What's going on?"

Dr. Samuels placed his hand on Tyler's back and guided him toward the nearest waiting room. Both were seated on wooden chairs, upholstered in bright blue fabric. "Tyler, has your mother spoken to you about her condition?"

"No, not so much. But I can tell she's getting worse. Can you please tell me what's happening to her?"

"I was hoping Beth would do that herself, but at this point you have a right to know. A few weeks ago, we determined that she had reached a 'point of no return' with her cancer."

"What does that mean?" Tyler wondered as the color drained from his face.

"It means she probably isn't going to get any better. The cancer has advanced and is now beginning to affect her brain. From this point on, she's not going to be the woman you've known. There will probably be moments of lucidity, but I must warn you that she will think and act very differently. I just wanted you to prepare for it. It's become quite noticeable the last couple of days. I'm so sorry, Tyler."

Tyler nodded and Dr. Samuels walked away as purposely as before, without the slightest trace of emotion. Tyler figured that delivering such awful news was an occupational hazard and that it was the only way physicians could deal with such anguish on a regular basis. However, it seemed the exact tone of voice one uses to order a hamburger at a fast-food restaurant.

For all intents and purposes, he was proclaiming a death sentence for his mother; and it had all the warmth and empathy of an IRS audit.

He steeled himself in preparation for what he would find in room 532. Rounding the corner and entering the door, he saw his mother with an IV on each arm, her head to one side, and her appearance surprisingly disheveled. She was asleep, and Tyler was tempted to have her remain that way. He wasn't ready for this but decided to see what he could do to help her in this state.

"Mom? You awake?"

Irritatedly, Beth scrunched her face, roused herself, and began to mumble. "What is it?" she asked, her eyes still fully shut.

"Mom, it's me. I came to see you."

Beth opened her eyes thinly, as if beholding light for the first time in weeks. "Who?" she asked harshly.

"It's Tyler. I came by to check on you. How ya doin'?"

This was killing him. The mention of his name did nothing to push away the emotional clouds that had gathered and rested upon her.

"Awful! How do you think I'm doing?"

For the first time in his life, he had no idea what to say to his mother. It was as if he were stuck in a room greeting strangers and trading agonizing small-talk. Her terse answer eliminated all conversation along medical lines. It was also clear that the television in her room had been set more for the nurses than the patient. A trashy talk show was playing at full volume – some highly-devolved family in which all the women were pregnant and all the wrong men were responsible, or something like that. There was no way his mother would want this playing in her room. Though not his personal choice, he wished the Christian television network were available. She liked that stuff, he thought. He walked over and changed the channel to a news station rather than turn it off. He thought he needed the extra noise in the room. Bringing the volume down, he returned and sat next to his mother's bed.

Tyler decided to launch into a monologue to relieve the tension. "Yeah, so I was able to switch shifts with a guy at work, so it looks like I'll be able to see you Christmas Eve and Christmas. Isn't that great? The restaurant has been so crazy lately. Lots of corporate parties, which are the absolute worst to work. Those people get drunk out of their minds. It's like they've been freed from prison for six hours to experience as much revelry and debauchery as possible until they're returned to captivity. They are good tippers, though." Tyler mischievously smiled as he looked over to see if she got the joke.

Beth would only let go with an occasional "Mmm hmm" every so often, her eyes still mostly closed. Tyler would do what he could to keep the performance going, but he petered out after 15 minutes. Seeing her still on the verge of sleep, he decided to watch the news channel instead. About every minute or so, he would look over at his mother to see if there were any signs of awareness. Seeing none, he would look back to the TV screen.

After an hour or more of this stalemate, Beth suddenly uttered, "Be sure to buy something nice for Christopher."

Tyler hadn't heard that name in a very long time. She didn't even open her eyes to say it and immediately retreated into her silent cocoon. It was all too much to handle, in spite of the doctor's warning. He decided to leave, figuring she probably wouldn't know of his presence anyway. Putting on his coat and staring at her again for a few moments, he turned and headed for the door.

"Tyler, I want you to know that I'm praying for you."

The young artist stopped, turned and looked back. He hoped that when he did, she would be sitting up again, fire-eyed, and determined. Maybe it was all an elaborate ruse, a practical joke or ploy to see how much her son loved her. Having satisfied the requirements, she would be all made up, smiling, and say something like, "Gotcha!" It wasn't to be. She remained in her semi-conscious state. Tyler later decided that it was a brief moment of clarity from his cherished caretaker who believed in and practiced prayer quite regularly. "Thanks, Mom" was all he could utter in response as he left the room.

Cancer sucks. This was the extent of Tyler's journal entry for December 25 last year. He spent the better part of an hour staring at the journal page, tapping its surface with the non-writing end of his pen, but nothing else came to mind. This was the first Christmas without the tree, trimmings, and all the intangibles his mother provided to make the holiday so special. Never did he imagine that he would spend Christmas in the cancer ward of St. Luke's. After seeing his mother in decline, he decided to work on Christmas Eve, knowing that Christmas Day would be agonizing enough. Although she probably didn't know the difference, he was feeling guilty for not being with her the day before, but it was so difficult seeing her mental capacities compromised. He hated these lose/lose situations and the disease that brought it about. He also seemed to be forming a detachment to the One he believed allowed it to happen. He authoritatively closed the leather-covered book, picked up the present, and began the hundred-block drive to the hospital.

Upon arrival, Tyler decided to enter the room with gusto as opposed to the subtlety he had shown on his most recent visits. Maybe he could snap her out of whatever had overwhelmed her.

"Merry Christmas, Mom!"

Beth was in her usual heavily medicated state, eyes closed, with only the beeps and sweeps of machines providing background noise. His enthusiasm seemed to jolt her awake. She looked derisively toward her intruder. "What? Who is it?"

Tyler wondered how many people in scrubs and lab coats entered and exited this room daily. To her, he was nothing more than an orderly changing out a bedpan or a nurse checking her IV connection. "It's me, Mom! Tyler." Beleaguered, Beth uttered a faint moan, saying something inaudible. Tyler placed the gift on the chair near her bedside and stood over her, near her face. "I came to see you today. After all, it is Christmas."

Maybe because of the holiday she cherished so much, Beth seemed to be fighting to be *compos mentis* for her visitor this day. Inarticulately, she said, "Oh, that's nice of you. Thanks for coming." It was all she could do to keep her eyes open.

Tyler, trying to find some way to be festive in such a sterile environment, took the remote control from the nightstand and flipped through channels until he came to one that was playing Christmas music. It wasn't exactly the Ramsey living room, but maybe it would bring some good memories back.

"What is that racket?" Beth bellowed. "Turn that off!"

Tyler had already crossed the line and displeased her. Beth didn't have a crotchety bone in her body, so he felt awful eliciting that kind of raw emotion from her. Feeling personally rebuffed, he pressed the On/Off button and placed the remote control back on the nightstand.

Things were looking bleak with the likely potential to get worse. Only one thing could change the momentum. Grabbing the gift, Tyler said, "Hey Mom! I brought you a Christmas present."

"Hmmm?"

"I said I brought you a Christmas present. See?"

This forced her to open her eyes and focus on something besides her pain or the drugs nullifying it. "What's that, a present?"

"Yeah. For you."

Surprisingly, Beth did what she could to aright herself in bed, which wasn't much. "Can you open it for me?"

Even in her depleted state, Tyler wasn't expecting his mother to be too weak to open a poorly wrapped package. "Uh, sure Mom. You ready?" Beth made no indication whether she was or not, so Tyler began unwrapping.

He was very proud of his selection. Knowing how much Beth used her beloved King James Bible, he thought buying her something updated would be just the answer. Pages had been falling out of hers for years, and she had vowed that she would get herself a new one soon; but she never got around to it. Now he had bought her a parallel Bible, containing two versions of the Bible side-by-side: her usual King James and a more up-to-date translation to its right. It had a light brown leather cover with her name inscribed on the front. Tyler had also taken the time to write a dedication on the inside cover in calligraphy. He remembered how she had written down the date of his conversion in his Bible years ago. He thought this would be a unique way of returning the favor. He was tempted to tell her about it but decided to let it be a surprise whenever she got around to looking through it.

"Look, Mom! It's a parallel Bible."

"A what?" She would normally never have to ask that.

"It's a new Bible with two versions next to each other. I thought you'd really love it for your devotional times." He did everything but place the Bible in her hands. He wasn't going to let her lie there and moan her way through it. He desperately wanted this to be a Christmas still worth remembering.

Struggling to open her eyes and grasping the gift her son had put atop the blanket near her stomach, she picked it up and began turning some pages. Tyler realized it was the first time he had seen the pupils of her eyes in weeks. He had almost forgotten what color her eyes were.

"What the hell is this?"

Tyler was aghast. His mother was so prim and proper that the only time he could remember her cursing was when his father's drunkenness drove her to total frustration. Had he now done the same to her? "Huh?" was all he could ask.

"I can't read this! The print's too small. Why did you give me this?"

He never remembered her having issues with her vision before, so he was completely caught off guard by her indictment. He felt like a five-year-old caught eating from the cookie jar before dinner. By instinct, he began backpedaling, looking and searching for an explanation for his behavior. His natural self-preservation then gave way to finding an alternate solution to the problem. If there was one thing Tyler couldn't accept, it was anyone else being unhappy. "Uh, well, what if I got you a magnifying glass? Would that help?"

"A what? I don't know," she muttered as she lay back down to her original position, leaving the new Bible open on top of the blanket.

Tyler wasn't going to be right until he fixed this. His heart raced in a desperate attempt to bandage what he had caused. "Tell you what, I will head down to the gift shop and see if they have a magnifying glass down there, OK?"

Beth could only moan her reply. Tyler scampered abruptly out of the room and fast-walked to the elevator. He was treating this like a timed event. He desperately wanted her to love this gift and no imposition was too great to see it through. He didn't want to let her down. Forgetting what day it was, he was disappointed to find the gift shop closed. His heart sank as he stared at the darkened, glassed-in space. Finding a chair in a quiet corner of the mostly deserted lobby, he sat and stared at the floor, yielding to his perpetual feelings of personal failure. He wondered if it might have been his biggest blunder yet. *How could I be so insensitive? She could barely keep her eyes open as it was. What made me think she was going to do any reading?* He mentally bludgeoned himself for the better part of an hour before deciding to return to the fifth floor empty-handed.

Reentering the room, he saw Beth exactly as he had left her an hour before. Though she may have been none the wiser, her son was determined to right his wrong at the first opportunity. Standing over her bed again, Tyler said, "First thing tomorrow morning, I'm going to get you that magnifying glass, OK?"

Beth showed no signs of acknowledgment, lying still with her eyes closed. Tyler felt out of options. His strategy to salvage Christmas as a family had failed. He had no more Christmas magic to offer. After staring at his mother for the better part of 20 minutes and seeing she was not going to be alert anytime soon, Tyler took his leave. He put the Bible on her nightstand so it would not be an impediment for the nurses and headed out the door.

Upon entering his car and driving through the mostly empty parking garage, Tyler chose complete silence to accompany him on his drive home. He wasn't about to listen to Christmas music, or any music for that matter. He didn't want to hear anything. Unfortunately for Tyler, he chose to think. He replayed those uncomfortable moments with the Bible repeatedly and even hours later. He questioned every decision he had made about the gift and about the visit. If only he had thought things through. If only he had taken her condition into account, this could have been a far better Christmas.

Just over two weeks later, as Tyler was sitting near the back of First Community's sanctuary on a frigid Sunday morning, he could feel his cell phone vibrating in his front pants pocket. As he pulled out the phone during Pastor Wilkins' sermon, a handful of people around him looked over in curiosity or disdain, depending upon the person. He noticed an unfamiliar number with a 216 area code. He politely excused himself from the room, walked into the lobby of the church, and received the call.

"Hello?" he said with an inescapable echo in this grand, old room.

"Yes, I am trying to teach Tyler Ramsey. Are you Tyler?"

Tyler wondered why any company would be calling him on Sunday morning, attempting to make a sale. The only people who would be awake for such a call would be in church. He was tempted to hang up, but the local phone number of the caller intrigued him. "Yes it is."

"Tyler, this is Dr. Samuels from St. Luke's Hospital."

The young man prepared himself for the worst but said nothing.

"Tyler, are you there?"

"Yes, I'm here."

"I wanted to call to say that your mother took a turn for the worse last night."

Tyler immediately began walking to his car while holding the phone up to his left ear. Most of the year, he could walk to the church, but January on Lake Erie was no time to be a hero. "What happened?"

"Basically, the cancer has advanced to a point at which she probably has only 24 hours to live."

Dr. Samuels continued his dissertation, but it became muffled in Tyler's mind with the phrase "24 hours to live". His mind raced in multiple directions. *Was that a guess or a medical certainty?* Tyler was picking up certain phrases: "keeping her comfortable," "need to make arrangements," and "machines doing most of the work."

Tyler was in the driver's seat of his vehicle when he finally spoke next, "OK. I understand."

"I'm very sorry, Tyler, but I wanted you to know as quickly as possible."

As he put his phone down on the passenger seat, Tyler didn't know what to do except go to the hospital. He stopped off at the loft and changed into more comfortable clothes. On his way to St. Luke's, he left a message at Calvary Fellowship. Then he called Adam and Rita, his uncle and aunt, delegating them to call whatever other family they thought needed to know. After parking in the hospital garage and walking through the familiar hallways, he emerged from the elevator on the fifth floor. After what he had seen the previous weeks, he wondered how much worse his mother could look.

Entering Room 532, he realized the answer to his unspoken question was "much worse." Lying on her back, hair strewn about, unbrushed for days, mouth hanging open like an elderly nursing-home patient without her dentures, Beth seemed attached to so many machines and contraptions that she almost didn't seem human. Her "breathing" was more the manipulation of external gizmos than an involuntary expansion of the lungs. With every breath, she looked as if someone in the ceiling were pulling on puppet strings, jerking her slightly upward and back down again. She had become a half-creature, a bad science-fiction movie's conception of a robot.

He couldn't even approach her bed. He leaned against the opposite wall, near the door, and found it difficult to even keep his eyes on her. He didn't know where Elizabeth Ramsey was, but she was nowhere near this place. This grotesque shell before him was nothing but a ruined carcass. He could not stay in there any longer. Exiting the room, he jogged to the same nearby waiting room in which he was first told that his mother was going to die weeks before. He was relieved to see the room empty. He knew it wouldn't be for long as relatives would be crowding him, patronizing him, filling him with ridiculous clichés and hackneyed maxims that belonged on religious tchotchkes. He wasn't ready for any of it. He leaned his head back against the wall and stared out the large window opposite him. He wanted to cry, but preparing to receive the throng of visitors diverted his emotional attention.

They would begin to arrive within the hour. All of them well-meaning; most of them woefully inadequate to the task. They would find Tyler in the waiting room, embrace him, say something trite, walk into the hospital room to see Beth, and rejoin Tyler in the waiting room for more forced conversation. Tyler felt the obligation of keeping his extended family engaged and informed. To minimize unwanted attention, he tried to appear as content as possible, even offering an occasional humorous line to alleviate the tension.

Later in the afternoon, it was his Uncle Adam who first referred to his mother in the past tense. "I tell you, she was a great lady." Tyler privately resented the fatalistic tone of the comment but made no outward signs of displeasure. By 8 p.m., there were about 15 people in the waiting room with Tyler, most of them having their own conversations. He had stared at the magazines nearby so long that he had memorized the titles of all the featured articles mentioned on each cover. He was never alone for more than a few minutes as those gathered believed this to be the worst thing for him. Tyler didn't have the heart to tell them he wished they would all leave.

Later in the evening, his aunt Rita approached him and broached a difficult subject. "Tyler, I know this is rather morbid, but have you thought at all about the arrangements for your mom?"

"A little bit."

"OK. Is it all right if we talk about that?" Rita was always more concerned about what was around the corner than about what was presently happening. It made her seem insensitive, which was appropriate since that seemed to be her nature. "Did your mom have anything prepared ahead of time?"

"Like...?"

"Like a burial plot or coffin. Things like that."

She wasn't dead yet, and they were already burying her. "I don't think she did. Mom was always confessing her healing, believing the Lord was going to keep her alive to see her grandchildren. The possibility that she might die never seemed to enter her mind."

"Oh. I see," Rita replied, trying to make sense of it.

"I know she didn't have very much. That house was just about the only asset she had." Tyler paused for about a half-minute as he weighed his options. "I think she would probably want to be cremated."

Rita was taken aback. No one on Beth's side of the family had done so, and to her it seemed an odd choice. "Well, Tyler, we can certainly help with the cost of a plot..."

"No," Tyler interrupted, "she never wants a big fuss made over her. She is not about drawing attention to herself. She likes to keep things simple. She wouldn't want a State funeral with all the trappings. She'd be mad if I did that." The irony of the statement was lost on Tyler. "We'll do a memorial service at Mom's church. I'm sure they'll take care of a meal and put together a nice service for her."

"OK, honey," Rita said. It was the most affectionate she would ever be with him, so much so that it was unnerving. "We know a funeral home that handled your grandmother's service. They can meet with you to pick out an urn for the ashes."

"Yeah. All right," Tyler said abruptly.

"Well, I just wanted to check with you before everything starts happening. Please know that your uncle and I are here to help in any way."

It was always difficult to ascertain the genuineness of his Aunt Rita. Though she and his mother were sisters, they were often on opposite sides of many debates and quarrels. He remembered them battling one another over funeral details when their mother died a few years before. They rarely got along, so any sign of warmth on her part had to be viewed with great skepticism. She was the master of ulterior motives. "Thanks. I appreciate it," Tyler said.

"No problem. By the way, did your mother have a will?"

The mask of feigned concern was slipping. He wondered whether to brand her a hyena or vulture. "Uh, she might have. At her last church a few years ago, they had somebody in who helped people put together wills. Mom was sick at the time and thought it might be a good idea."

Rita's face brightened. "Oh, that's a relief!"

Definitely a vulture. "Yeah, but I'm not sure what's in it. It's not like there's a huge estate to settle."

"Well, as long as you don't lose the house."

The house. That was it. Suddenly, even in the midst of distress, Tyler connected the dots. Adam and Rita's son Kevin was nearing thirty but showed no signs of launching out on his own. He was perennially unemployed and devoted much of his energies to achieving new high scores in whatever video game he was trying to master at the time. It was the house they wanted. They wanted a place for their son to go. Unbelievable. "I suppose so," Tyler said.

Even Rita knew better than to press further. Looking at her cell phone, she exhaled deeply and said, "Well, I guess we should be going."

Yes, you should. "Well, thanks for coming. I know Mom would appreciate it."

Patting his knee as she stood, Rita replied, "Well, we just really appreciate you, too, sweetheart. Let us know if there's anything we can do."

Tyler surely had an answer, but being a Christian prohibited him from expressing it. "Will do," he chose instead.

The waiting room emptied out quickly after that. On their way out, most of the assembled would ask some derivative of, "Do you need us to stay with you? Because we can, you know. We can stay here all night if you need us to." All the while, Tyler knew they were hoping and praying that he would say, "No. That's OK. I'll call you if there's any change," and they would be on their way.

At midnight, he was alone again. He had not seen his mother since he first arrived over twelve hours before. He knew he would have to go back in there at some point. Should he sit at her bedside until she died? Was that the valiant thing to do? Could he possibly look at her in that state for that long? What if the doctor was wrong? What if this went on for days or weeks? What if the doctor was right? That meant she could be gone at any moment.

Tyler felt he was forever being put in these situations of everything being the wrong thing. Going over his options for almost an hour, he finally decided that he would go home and come back in the morning. However, he knew he needed to walk to Room 532 again before he did.

Nothing had changed in his mother's appearance. None of the family members dared say it, but Tyler thought she looked positively freakish. He now wanted it to be over. He didn't need these images marring the mental scrapbook he had formed of her. Like his previous visit, he leaned against the back wall, almost afraid he would awaken her and hear God knows what coming from her mouth. He hoped for her unconsciousness to continue.

The beeps and tones from the Stonehenge of machines that seemed to surround her provided an odd soundtrack for what was becoming an increasingly uncomfortable moment. Should he say something to her? Things like that always happened on television. Nothing came to mind. She wouldn't have heard him anyway. Or would she? He remembered reading something about how patients in surgery can still hear what their doctors are saying, and it can affect their prognosis if positive things are being said. Maybe this was one of those situations. But "Get better, Mom" seemed a bit ridiculous at this point. Something told him that the doctor was right and that this was probably going to be the last time he saw her. Each second made him increasingly tongue-tied. Stepping slightly forward from the wall, he put on his winter coat, looked one more time at the final ravages of breast cancer, said, "Goodbye, Mom" and left for his car.

During the brief ride home and lying in bed that night, Tyler could not get that frightful, freakish picture of his mother's artificial breathing out of his head. She had been transformed into a marionette, he reasoned. Then he began to ponder on Who was really pulling the strings. Why was He allowing her to live like this, even for a few days or weeks? Why was He taking such delight in seeing her suffer? She had served Him faithfully, asking for nothing. She had endured alcoholism from her parents and her ex-husband. She didn't deserve this. Tyler continued to ponder the injustice of it all until exhaustion finally turned to slumber.

He would get the call at 5:30 a.m. Someone on the staff at St. Luke's called to inform him that his mother had passed away at 5:08. Tyler offered his thanks and began the process of memorializing his mother. The problem was that he had never begun the process of grieving her.

Eleven

It was the first time Tyler had replayed those horrible events in his mind in eleven months. As he slowly shifted from memory back to present observation, he focused again on the finished Christmas tree. He thought about those hours leading up to and the days following the demise of his relationship with his mother. As he reflected upon it, he found himself infused with great regret. He was clearly more concerned with how others were feeling and doing than he was with his own well-being. At the viewing and memorial services, he was more of a host than a grieving son. He knew everyone would be watching him for some chink in the armor, some sign that he was losing control. He refused to give anyone the pleasure. On the contrary, he was engaging and friendly far beyond his normal personality, even exchanging jokes with people to lighten the mood. He wanted people leaving those occasions saying, "Now that's one strong kid." Privately, he decided he would take care of himself later. After all, wasn't that the Christian thing to do?

The funeral transitioned quickly into handling the will and estate, which meant deciding what to do with the house and all the possessions in it. Keeping the title of the house, Tyler's prediction came true as he put his mother's things into storage and his cousin Kevin moved in to continue his Peter Pan approach to life. However, having someone there meant the utilities were taken care of and the yard was looked after. Tyler was relieved he didn't have to deal with it. There wasn't anything else of value in his mother's possession. By the time it was all settled, he was ready to get back to his normal life.

This Christmas Eve night had revealed that the "later" of taking care of his wounds had still not come yet, but maybe it wasn't needed. Maybe Tyler was doing such a great job of adjusting that he didn't need to experience what others did after a loss. He thought he must have prepared himself well for her death. Then he remembered being rejected by his girlfriend and the reasons why. He considered that he had almost no people within his inner circle. With Shelly out of the picture, his entire support system was made up of people at work and a couple twice his age from his church. Isn't this what he had been frustrated with his mother for doing? Maybe he hadn't prepared so well after all.

He could not stop thinking about Beth's last night of life and his reluctance to approach her. He would never have that chance again. There were so many things unsaid. She didn't even have a burial site where he could go and even pretend to speak to her. Maybe journaling would do the trick. He was about to stand up from the couch and retrieve his journal and pen when he looked down and realized that he was still holding the gift Bible from the church open on his lap. It seems he had completed the journey to Matthew 2 at some point, but he couldn't remember when. "As long as I'm here," he said aloud and began reading the chapter.

Jesus was born in Bethlehem in Judea, during the reign of King Herod. About that time some wise men from eastern lands arrived in Jerusalem, asking, "Where is the newborn king of the Jews? We saw his star as it rose, and we have come to worship him.

He put the Bible down for a moment and looked at the Christmas tree, reflecting on what he had just read. This was exactly why Tyler was never a fan of most Bible reading plans. He thought he read the Bible too slowly. The artist within him would take over, and he would often put the Bible down and create the picture of the scene in his mind. By the time he would return to the text, 15-20 minutes would elapse. He never told anyone about his eccentric method, as many of his religious friends were books ahead of him. He thought about the Magi and the star that celestially served as a beacon for their journey. To be so convinced that a formation in the heavens could be a creation of God intended for only a few people seemed baffling. He looked at the tree and wondered why he didn't have stories like that. Whenever his mother would watch Christian television, there was always someone on there speaking right to the camera or in an interview about those God-ordained moments when they were seated next to the high priest of the Satanist church or something and, by the time the plane touched down, the guy had been converted and somehow water-baptized. Tyler never had stories like that. Of course, being seated next to the head of the Satanist church would have caused him to lose bladder control. No wonder he didn't have stories like that. I guess that's how they determine who is invited to be featured on Christian television – people who have stories like that.

He envied the Wise Men and the story they would be able to tell their children and grandchildren. To take the ultimate risk like that. What if the star stopped appearing halfway into their journey? Would somebody have just said, "Whoops! Sorry folks," and turned everyone around and returned home in shame? He figured that could have happened, but they decided to take a holy gamble. "Hmm," Tyler said, very proud of the phrase he had conjured. "They took a holy gamble." He reasoned that their journey happened because of what they had observed and what they had believed. Tyler was getting filled with excitement. It had been a long time since he had taken the time to read and ponder the Word of God this way. *They saw something which confirmed something they believed, and they acted on it.* That was it. He wished he had something like that experience to remember.

Tyler analyzed that last thought as he stared at the tree. Then his mind drifted off to consider what the star must have looked like. What was it about its shape, size, or brilliance that convinced them that this was a divine message specifically for them? Somewhere in the transition of thinking of the star and beholding the tree, he was suddenly made aware of a glaring omission.

"The star!" Tyler said excitedly, as he shot up from the couch, laying the Bible aside on the cushion. He had neglected to put the star tree-topper on the Christmas tree. Racing over to the bins, he fished through layers of unused decorations, bypassing place settings, napkins, candy jars, decorative bowls, candle holders, and even Yuletide towels that were set out in the kitchen and bathroom. Finally he found the white star. The cord was tangled with a few items, so extracting it took more finesse than Tyler was willing to display at this time of night. Having freed it from its Christmas coffin, Tyler beheld it like an unearthed precious jewel as a smile opened up broadly on his hopeful face. He had to find another extension cord to connect it to the power strip at the bottom of the tree. Thankfully, it lit up when it was plugged in. Tyler returned to his place on the sofa and was grateful for the sudden memory. "How could I have forgotten that?" The brightness of the white light contrasted nicely with the colored lights around the tree's body.

Tyler wasted no time in adding the star to his painting, making it the brightest feature of the scene, larger and even brighter than what shone in his apartment. As he finished, he wondered if the star of the Magi was like that; something unmistakable, even unavoidable.

Initially believing that the star-topper was the whole point of the scripture he just read, he returned to the sofa and realized that he still felt unsettled, especially as he considered the memories over his mother's passing. He picked up the Bible again and returned to Matthew 2, reading on.

After this interview the wise men went their way. And the star they had seen in the east guided them to Bethlehem. It went ahead of them and stopped over the place where the child was.

Tyler set the Bible down and began mentally painting the picture of the star and setting it against a normal evening sky. He figured it had to be at least triple the size of the others and just as bright. While others would have seen it as an anomaly of science, the sky-searchers would have known from their study of the Scriptures that something else was afoot. He wondered of their adventures and discussions along the way to Bethlehem. How far would they have to go? How long would it take?

Even as Tyler Ramsey thought of these wondrous things, he also knew that something seemed to be pulling him. While all of humanity slept in their beds with visions of sugar plums and all that, something was urging Tyler away from where he was. He wasn't sure if it was the power of suggestion from reading the Bible story or something else, but he had the palpable sense that he needed to go somewhere, even at this late hour.

Normally, Tyler would have submerged such feelings under an avalanche of logic and rationalization. However, he decided that he wasn't that guy right now. Bundling himself with a scarf, gloves, and his winter coat, he left the apartment and started walking, but he wasn't sure why or where. Taking the elevator down to the lobby, he walked out the front door onto one of Cleveland's downtown streets. It was quiet. Tyler thought the only people awake, besides himself, were thousands of unfortunate moms and dads around the world trying to assemble bikes before their children woke up.

He could feel the cold, crisp air as he had hours before. His building faced north toward Lake Erie, so when he realized there was still no wind, he was thankful it wouldn't impair his ability to complete this quest, whatever it was. He looked down the street in each direction at the politically-correct street decorations meant to depict Christmas but not depict Christmas. Poles along the avenue alternated between lit depictions of holly, Santa Claus, and candles. Tyler thought about how Beth would make a statement each year about how the country was slowly taking the "Christ" out of Christmas and her personal crusade to turn the tide. She would get really worked up about articles she had read or news reports she had heard on TV until she realized she had neither the power nor the time to do much about it, and she would let it go at that.

There he stood, unsure of what to do next. He was like a kid learning to roller skate, unwilling to let go of the safety bar and skate in the middle of the floor. All he could see beyond the street decorations and blinking signal lights was his own breath in the chilly Cleveland air. Then the familiar Tyler caught up with the adventurous one standing on a sidewalk at 2 a.m. *What are you doing here? You look ridiculous! Get inside before you catch pneumonia.* Feelings of insecurity and humiliation weren't far behind. He knew them well. What was he doing anyway? Was he so desperate for something beyond himself that he had talked himself into this misadventure? Maybe he should stop before he was spotted by someone else.

As he considered going back inside, he looked up in what could only be described as complete frustration and finally spotted it. Above him, to his right was something he had never noticed before. Above the tall office buildings and above the aeronautical path of helicopters and planes was something large, luminescent, and beyond description. Tyler was amazed that anything could shine that brightly against the heat and activity of a metropolitan area. He was no astronomical expert, and he wasn't sure if the local news had spoken of being able to see some kind of comet or planet tonight, but this was the most beautiful star he had ever seen. He was filled with an odd mixture of child-like innocence and adult-onset cynicism. "Come on!" he even said to the empty street. "Are you kidding me?"

He recalled what had propelled him out here only minutes before. *They saw something which confirmed something they believed, and they acted on it.* As he beheld the wonder in the sky, he knew he was at another point of decision. Was this really what he thought it might be? He couldn't remember a moment in recent memory when he was more excited. He shook his head when he remembered the scripture and how the star was east of where he now stood. "God, what am I supposed to do here?" he whispered, fearful of anyone within earshot hearing. Halfway expecting an audible voice to speak, he instead was overwhelmed by a pervasive thought to follow it. *Follow it?* What was his next instruction going to be, "Find a camel"?

Deciding he had come too far to turn back, he walked to the parking garage, got in his car, and, emerging from the entrance, leaned forward in the driver's seat and looked out the top of the windshield to see if the star was still there. It was. He drove into its direction. After about five blocks, he wondered how long this was going to be. After all, stars are seen by the entire world. Was he going to be driving east all night? He'd end up in Pennsylvania or even New York by daybreak. He didn't have the gas money to be a Wise Man.

Another ten blocks and Tyler pulled off to the side of the street and got out of his car. It was too difficult to both observe the star and drive safely, even on deserted streets. Shutting the car door, he looked up again to the heavens. Not only was the star there but it seemed slightly larger than it had been back at his apartment building. He got back into his car and repeated the process ten blocks later. Again, the cosmic wonder was larger, but this time it also appeared closer to the horizon.

By his fourth repetition, Tyler knew his final destination. Though he daily traversed the downtown streets of Cleveland, he knew this commute better than any. He remained in his car for another fifty-plus blocks, pulled in to the emergency room parking lot of St. Luke's Hospital, turned off the ignition, and stepped out of his vehicle. The star was twice the size of the moon and seemed to be suspended directly over the hospital. Accessing the hospital through the emergency room was different than his usual routine but not unfamiliar. He needed no instruction or direction. He knew where he was going. Pushing "5" on the column of elevator buttons, he almost held his breath as the car ascended, finally opening up to the floor that had been the site of great loss and pain.

He didn't know what he was to do, only where he was supposed to do it; and now he was here again for the first time since the day of his mother's death. As he remembered it, he had come by later that morning at the hospital's request to collect a box of Beth's personal items. An administrator of some sort handed it to him, sealed with packing tape, and the name "Ramsey" quickly scribbled in black marker on the side.

Walking quietly through the darkened hallway, he did his best not to attract undue attention. Though it had been a year, the mixed scent of death and disinfectant still hung palpably in the air. Knowing the lay of the land, he found a way to avoid the central nurse's station on the floor and avoid detection. He knew no better place to go than Room 532. Arriving there, he noticed that the door was slightly ajar, keeping light out for the sleeping patient but allowing the nurses easy access to administer medicine or change IVs.

Before nudging the door open so he could fit through and enter, he looked at the nameplate just under the room number. It said, "DiGrassi." Rather than enter, he stopped himself, sensing that this wasn't the room he was supposed to enter. *Why wouldn't it be this room?* he wondered. Still, he couldn't shake it. He wasn't supposed to go in there. So where was he supposed to go? Maybe he had made this whole thing up in his head? Maybe he had assumed things about the star that really weren't true? What was it about this place that brought him so much confusion?

He continued walking toward the end of the hall. Stopping at Room 530, he saw the name "Gilford" written in temporary marker. That room didn't feel right either. "Where's your precious star now?" an evil part of Tyler's mind seemed to be saying to him. He was tempted to flee the scene, but he resisted and continued tiptoeing down the hallway. Looking back over his shoulder, he made sure no medical professionals were wise to his movements. He wondered what would happen if he were caught. Was this a crime? Could he get in trouble for this? He reasoned that as long as he didn't unplug anything, he was in the clear.

Reaching #528, he looked again on the nameplate and was intrigued by the name that was written: "BIRNBAUM." *Birnbaum? Could it be?* Looking behind him down the hallway once more and assured all was clear, he slowly pushed open the door to the room. Immediately returning the door to its original position so as not to raise suspicion, he looked at the room's occupant and, in the darkness, could not quite make out specifics. Leaning against the back wall, he initially couldn't even decipher the gender of the patient. However, by the time his eyes fully adjusted, he knew it was a woman by the trinkets and gifts that had been bought for her.

It had been many years since he had last seen Violet Birnbaum. Occasionally, he would ride his bike past her house and yell hello to her while she weeded her garden. Tyler couldn't remember if he had been in her house since the night Christopher died. He wasn't sure why. Was this Violet? Whoever it was, she wasn't so much asleep as heavily sedated. Tyler knew the difference. Finding a flower bouquet on the window ledge, he looked and discovered a card attached to a toothpick-like mechanism stuck in the soil. Pulling it out, it was difficult to ascertain the penmanship in this light. Pulling out his cell phone and facing the corner of the room with his back to the patient to provide a shield to prevent illumination in the rest of the room, he activated it; and the glow of the phone provided the assistance he was looking for. "Violet, we love you and are praying for you." The card was signed, "Your church family at Trinity." Putting everything back where it belonged, his confirmation was complete.

Leaning against the back wall again, he stared at what remained of Violet Birnbaum, pondering his next move. It was all too familiar. Beholding a woman who now was more machine than human seemed eerily reminiscent. He didn't know her diagnosis, but he could guess her prognosis. This would be her last Christmas. He wondered if her family knew that or whether they were holding out hope. He wondered if Violet had changed in her demeanor and said nasty things to her kids in her haggard state. Were any of her relatives angling for her house behind the scenes?

And why was he here anyway? Certainly he wasn't here to merely observe. Was he supposed to wait for something else to happen? Would there be an angelic visitation? He didn't believe himself worthy of or ready for that. One thing he did remember is his last hours with his mother and how he couldn't seem to free himself from a wall just like this one. Whatever he was supposed to do, this wall had nothing to do with it. He had spent the last 11 months trying to get off that wall and, by God, he was going to do it.

Removing his coat and stepping toward the patient, he sat in a high-backed chair near her bed, no doubt intended for patients who needed to get out of bed just to change position. He looked at her face for many minutes, trying to recall what it should have looked like. She always seemed to have an air of dignity about her. While in no way snobbish, she almost seemed more worthy of a stately home than the average abode in which she resided. He remembered her to be a classy lady, always polite, presentable and well-attired. He could see vestiges of her former glory, but they were greatly obscured. She had no part in this display.

This whole exercise was doing no good. Surely he hadn't come down here simply to witness the death of someone else he knew. What was the point in that? "See Tyler? It happens to lots of people." Was this the message the Lord was trying to convey? He looked at her again for a few moments. Staring at her face, he thought about all she was and represented to him and others. So caught up in emotion was he that he began speaking to her.

"Hi, Mrs. Birnbaum. It's me, Tyler Ramsey. Not sure if you remember me or not."

Tyler stopped himself, overcome by a sudden torrent of awkwardness. He wanted to go back to the wall again or even leave the room altogether. Was he really choosing to speak to a woman who had been medicated into unconsciousness? This is usually the point at which Tyler Ramsey could talk himself out of anything. He decided to reach deeper into the well of his heart, past the fear of failure or ridicule, deeper than the flight response and self-preservation that seemed to cloud his daily activities.

"I didn't know you were here. I'd love to sit here and say that I heard and just had to get down here right away to see you, but I honestly didn't know until minutes ago. I'm sorry you have to go through this. I won't be so insensitive as to say I know what you're going through, but I have seen this pretty close-up. I can only hope it ends mercifully for you."

Tyler recoiled at his own morbidness. Why was he saying this to a patient?

"Anyway, I came by your room and saw your name on the door and just had to see if it was you. I hope you're doing OK."

Violet remained motionless in her pharmaceutically-induced state as Tyler continued.

"You know, I haven't been here for almost a year. It was just a couple of doors down that..."

The dreaded sentence. For once, the young man didn't overthink something. He didn't overanalyze a statement before it left his mouth. He just spoke without parsing every syllable, and he walked right into it.

"...that Mom died." He leaned back in the chair and sighed. Running his hand through his light-brown hair and closing his eyes, he knew what he had to do. He decided to leave his eyes shut while he spoke for the time being.

"I often go back to that night in January and what I could have done differently. There you were looking almost inhuman, and there I was glued to the wall, afraid to approach you. I didn't know what to say or do. I wanted to be real heroic and look like the good son, but the truth is I never wanted to see you like that again. That's what I hate about this God-awful disease. It does nothing but take away and slowly at that. Every time I would walk into that room those last few weeks, there was at least one less piece of you. Every day, I knew that I would walk into this hospital and there would be less of you here than the day before. I can't even tell you how awful that was! Your memory and recognition got slower. One more slight hint of color would go out of your face. Less light would shine from your eyes. You underwent this metamorphosis from mother to stranger. It was a horrible, slow erosion. I know you were in unbelievable pain and anguish, but so was I!"

Tyler was raising his voice to a passionate level. He opened his eyes and remembered where he was. He didn't want to alert the staff or wake any patients, so he looked again at Beth's proxy and returned to uttering hushed tones.

"It got so that I would hold my breath from the parking lot to the room. At some point, I knew it wasn't going to get better. With each visit, I knew what awaited me behind the door was going to be worse than the day before. Why didn't you tell me that? Why did I have to hear it from some doctor? Why did you think I couldn't handle that?"

Again, Tyler's voice was getting louder. Realizing it, he shut his mouth and eyes in frustration, inwardly berating himself for getting carried away again. The problem was that the emotional magma within him was building to a formidable level, and he knew he couldn't turn back.

"Look, I know it isn't your fault, and you were just trying to protect me, but I had a right to know. I could have at least prepared myself for what was coming. Knowing you, you probably were still believing you were going to be healed, even to your last rational moment. I've never had your faith. I've believed in God, but I haven't had what you've had. You know me, the realist, always anticipating the worst.

"I don't see why you had to go. It's not that I wanted you to live with the pain, but I couldn't stand to lose one more thing."

Tyler's voice cracked as tears welled. He sat back in the chair and thought about his last statement. It said so much that desperately needed to be said. "I felt like I lost the only person in the world who really believed in me." Tears now overflowed from his eyes and down his cheeks. He made no effort to abate them. "There's nobody left who's proud of me." Though the current of tears was becoming intense enough to flow to his jaw line and drip onto his shirt, his hands remained in his lap. He wanted to feel the streams flowing and resting on his cheeks.

"I don't know who to love anymore. I don't know how to love anymore." Every statement was punctuated by long pauses and deep mourning. "I really wish you were here, because I don't seem to know what to do. For so long, it was just you and me looking out for each other. I tried to be the best son I could. Then when you got sick, I tried to take care of you. Then when you got really sick, I tried to visit and encourage you. And now that you're gone..."

Tyler initially buried his head in his hands, but he knew it wasn't enough. He took his coat, put it over his face, and began wailing into it. For a brief moment, he wondered if anyone could hear him, then he didn't care. He let go of months, even years of frustration and anguish. The intensity was such that only Tyler would have been able to decipher the actual words being said in those few moments when he spoke over his tears. "I'm so sorry, Mom! I'm so sorry!" Pleadingly, his voice raised at least an octave as he wept into his makeshift handkerchief. "Help me, Jesus! Please help me, Jesus!" From that point on, only tears would do. He had said all he could say and began to drain the emotional infection he had carried from his wounds for too long.

Twenty minutes later, he was finally at a point in which he could set the coat aside and look at Violet Birnbaum again. Though occasional tears would still appear, the ferocity of the torment had passed. He was almost weightless, wondering if he would even have the strength to stand if called upon. In the silence, he reflected upon many events, both recent and distant, and his place in all of them.

Once his composure fully returned, he knew it was time to go. As he stared at Violet, Tyler realized that once again she had been there for him at a difficult hour of need. A smile formed on his reddened face as he realized what he needed to do. Reaching into the front pocket of his coat, he pulled out the jewelry box that had been resting there for more than 24 hours. Finding a piece of scrap paper on her tray table and a black marker used for the erase board in her room, Tyler wrote the following:

To Violet:
Merry Christmas
from an old family friend

He placed the note underneath the jewelry box on the tray table, displaying it prominently so there would be no mistake of its intent. Walking toward her and bending down, Tyler kissed Violet on the forehead, causing her to twitch ever so slightly before returning to her almost comatose state.

Putting his coat back on, Tyler walked out of the room, pausing briefly to make sure the hallway was clear.

As he exited the facility and headed back to his car, Tyler couldn't remember feeling lighter. Maybe numb was a more apt word. For him, the circle was now complete. His journey had come to its rich end, and he was ready to sleep and face Christmas day with a greater sense of purpose and hope.

Until he saw the star again.

Twelve

It happened as Tyler started the ignition of his car. He noticed it once again. The magnitude of its brilliance was still dazzling. Its position was slightly higher than when he entered the hospital. Still, it was clearly visible through the top of his windshield. Tyler wondered whether it was a deified "tip of the hat" for a job well done in making the journey, an "atta boy" from God Himself.

Or maybe it still served a purpose. As Tyler exited the parking lot and began heading west toward his apartment building, he alternated his glance between the street and the star. Far from dissipating, it seemed to descend and expand as he progressed. About halfway home, the glowing orb once again seemed to hover over a predetermined spot, much like it had at St. Luke's. It then remained still, seemingly awaiting his arrival.

Tyler stopped at an intersection near East 40th Street. There was no discernible activity on the thoroughfare. Unsure of where to go or what to do, he parallel-parked along the street, put the car in "Park," and looked around for any clue as to why he was being sent on this errand. Not only was there no noticeable reason for this stop, but the star suddenly vanished. Somewhat panicked, Tyler shut off the engine, got out of the car, and looked in every conceivable direction for his cosmic guide, but it was gone.

Standing in the middle of the street, he sighed his frustration. Now what was he supposed to do? He considered returning home, wondering if his appointed rounds were now finished. Maybe he had made a wrong turn, and the star was so low that the next corner could once again reveal its presence. Deciding to continue on foot, he roamed downtown streets, craned his neck upward, and searched the visible Milky Way for any trace of what had been so obvious minutes before. It was a fruitless pursuit. Again, he questioned the reality of its appearance and intention, though he couldn't deny the results of following it earlier.

By the time he decided to end the search, he lowered his gaze and began massaging the back of his neck, now sore from continually looking upward. Taking note of his immediate surroundings, he had to admit that he was lost. He began searching for street signs in an effort to get his bearings. Jogging down the sidewalk of whatever road he was on, he hoped he could be within a climate-controlled environment soon. Though the winds were calm, this was still December in Cleveland.

Some of the business names on the street seemed familiar. Nearing the corner and reading the street sign above, he could safely guess he was about two blocks away from his vehicle. He was relieved and promised himself that his days of imitating Indiana Jones were over.

As he approached and rounded the corner, he beheld one of Cleveland's most historic churches. Emmanuel Church was an immense edifice. Its real estate nearly doubled that of First Community, occupying almost a full block. Built in the Gothic style, the building's most prominent feature was a tall copper steeple that rose 50 feet into the air. Even the night sky could not mask its beauty. Flanked by large floodlights, it was well-defined amidst its downtown neighbors. Tyler slowed his pace and even halted in the presence of such architectural magnificence. He had never seen the church at night. Then again, he hadn't really examined it in the daylight either. Now he was noticing everything with new significance.

Walking slowly to take in its full grandeur, he appreciated every inch of the place, much like beholding a national wonder or historic monument. Approaching the far corner of the structure and the end of its block, as he was ready to finally take his eyes off the place, he came upon one more display only a few feet in front of him. It was Emmanuel's nativity scene. Life-sized and brightly banked in blue floodlights, it featured all the traditional characters of the Christmas story. It was one of the largest displays of its kind that Tyler had ever seen.

It reminded him of something Grace Cathedral tried when he was a teenager. One holiday season, the church decided to undertake a live nativity in which cars would pull up to a designated part of the parking lot and actors would portray the roles of the essential Christmas players to a voice-over narration played over a weak radio signal. People would remain in their cars and enjoy the 20-minute presentation. The drama also included live animals like a donkey and a sheep. The church hoped it would be a unique outreach opportunity and raise its profile in the community. The results seemed to be mixed, however. Tyler remembered going with his mother one evening and watching in horror as the donkey, during the climactic manger scene, decided it was the perfect time to take care of some personal business right in front of the manger. Not wanting to waste an opportunity, Tyler looked at Beth and said, "I don't remember that scene from the Bible, do you?"

The memory made the young man chuckle as he stood on a city sidewalk in the middle of the night. No chance of that this evening, he figured. He stared at the enormous diorama. In the back left were the shepherds, looking in wonder and awe, holding shepherds' staffs and gesturing in the direction of the child. In front of them were a few sheep. To the back right were the Wise Men. Although Pastor Wilkins had reminded the church earlier that evening that they weren't present for this occasion, Tyler smiled as he looked at the three of them. They all wore crowns, were dressed in colorful robes, and carried treasure boxes. He could now relate to them in a whole new way.

In the foreground were the Holy family. Joseph and Mary, both with a slightly brighter countenance, knelt immediately before the food trough that had been manufactured into a makeshift crib for the King of Kings. From his vantage point, he could make out a hand barely reaching above the manger. He decided he wanted a closer look. As he did at the hospital, he looked in either direction to make sure no one was around or approaching. Seeing that the street was desolate and hearing no oncoming traffic, Tyler stepped off the sidewalk and onto the hardened sod of Emmanuel Church, approaching the scene.

Never at a loss for a contingency plan, he began devising an explanation should a police officer approach him, believing him to be a vandal or thief. He quickly realized no explanation would suffice. He hoped he had an innocent enough face to be believed. He surely couldn't say a star had (kind of) led him here. Who knows where that would land him? His internal panic device once again urged him to turn back and head home quickly, telling him that he had been lucky to this point, and his luck was going to run out. One more time, Tyler ignored the internal alarm and came upon the painted figures.

Placing his right hand on the back of the wise man farthest to the right, he could tell that these weren't ordinary store-bought decorations. There was a heft to them. They were solid, almost immovable. They could hold up to harsh Cleveland winds and the elements that ordinarily come with them. What really impressed him as an artist was the attention to detail. These had been hand painted, not mass produced. Expecting to see chipped paint upon closer inspection, he was surprised to notice individual brushstrokes on its face, robe, and crown. The same was true of each formidable piece of the display. Though the figures themselves were aged, the touch-up was recent. Someone took personal ownership of this.

Eyebrows had been fashioned in great detail. Fingernails were downright life-like. Nothing had been missed or passed over. No wonder it looked so beautiful.

Tyler was already glad he had taken the time to see this work of craftsmanship. How many thousands of people passed by this al fresco work of art daily without even a hint as to its authenticity? As an artist, Tyler knew that whoever had a hand in creating this didn't really care who noticed. He knew the reward was in the work itself. That's what the last 24 hours had reminded him. He needed to care less about selling and more about creating.

He saved his final inspection for the child. What had intrigued him the most when he first saw it was the fact that only the baby's hand was visible from the street. He thought that sent a beautiful message in many ways. It was a subtle reminder that even when we can't see Him, His hand is still reaching, still working on our behalf. Looking into the manger, he was somewhat surprised at what he saw. Most try to depict the infant Jesus as sullen, calm, and resting comfortably. That may have happened that night in Bethlehem, but Tyler was always bothered by that. Like any newborn, Jesus should have a restlessness about Him. In those conditions, heavenly visitations notwithstanding, He probably cried most of the night. For all the artistic renderings of a precious, holy bundle "asleep on the hay," he liked what he now saw. This baby was wide awake, almost fidgety, reaching for something...or Someone.

There was a clear glint in His eye, and the swaddling clothes meant to insulate Him from the elements had been agitated, almost kicked aside. He looked almost mischievous; not the usual rendering of the Messiah, but Tyler loved it. His smile broadened as he looked into the figure's face. Again, no detail had been bypassed. His mouth was agape, as if He had something important to say. *How appropriate*, Tyler thought. He had never seen anything like it. It was like discovering a completely new and wonderful side of a familiar friend's personality.

It was the first time Tyler Ramsey had ever seen Jesus Christ in more than one dimension. After all the sermons he heard, the personal Bible reading he undertook, and the prayers he uttered, he never felt closer to the Lord than he did now.

Only then did he realize how wrong his own picture of Him had been. For all his complaints about the way He was captured on canvas by other artists, it was clear now that Tyler had painted his own inaccurate depiction. Though he had never attempted to paint Him, in his mind, his Subject was anything but beautiful. He had imagined him with a fierce look of disdain and clenched fists in an attempt to resist the constant urge to exact vengeance upon Tyler for his constant misdeeds. He didn't know when that surrealistic sketching had initially formed within; but, as the years and disappointments went by, it had become imprinted on his heart. Every injustice and misfortune was viewed through that awful lens.

To Tyler, everything was payment for something; and, when he couldn't equate the two, it was laid at the feet of his God. It was a spiritualized version of Newton's Law: For every action, there is always an equal and opposite reaction. When something bad happened, it was probably because of something Tyler did. In those rare cases in which he couldn't blame himself, it was the Man in the cerebral painting taking delight in making him suffer for something he had done to someone, sometime somewhere.

The fallacy of all this became so clear as he looked upon one person's idea of Jesus. It may have been an opinion, but Tyler thought it was a good one. How could this beautiful infant become the awful taskmaster that permeated his thoughts and philosophy? How could this Ultimate Good morph into a false notion of someone out to get him? It was painful to have such a dark, untraveled corner of his heart illuminated for the first time. The shame of even believing such a lie at any point in his life made him want to run from the scene rather than be confronted by it. Two days ago, he would have done that.

Instead, Tyler sat cross-legged on the ground in front of the manger. His legs could instantly feel a cold chill through his thinly-layered dress pants. From this vantage point, he could barely see over the edge of the manger and to its holy contents. He sat in silence for many minutes. He was too overwhelmed to speak and too overcome to move. Wrapping his coat over his ears, mouth, and nose to protect him from the cold, he stared at the baby, replaying old events and the anger that had accumulated from them. Judging by his two-decades-plus of living, he wondered how many years had been wasted believing so many wrong things.

He had served and worshiped God at a distance for so long. To him, it was the safest place to be, away from His constant wrath. At this moment, however, he finally felt near to the Lord, physically and spiritually. He wished he had something akin to gold or frankincense or myrrh to bring. He had nothing like that, and it wasn't because of his poverty. He had been so angry for so long that, if he had been one of the Magi, the only thing he could have brought to Him was bitterness. He started to once again feel ashamed at his emptiness.

Just then Tyler had a novel thought. Placing his left arm on the top of the manger, he leaned forward until his forehead rested against it. With a gentle whisper, Tyler began to pray.

"Father..."

That word had always tripped him up. It had been the most puzzling word of the English language. He would sometimes jokingly say that the Lord's Prayer was his favorite scripture, except for the first two words of it. He wondered how many prayers had begun – and ended – with those two words over the course of his life. He couldn't let that happen now.

"Father...I...I...I don't really know what to say. I'm just...I'm just so sorry..."

Tyler clenched his fist, grabbing hold of the manger for support as he began to weep. He buried his eyes into the sleeve of his coat, waiting to catch his breath again until he could continue.

"I'm afraid I don't have much to bring you tonight. The Wise Men brought beautiful treasures from their land, all of them having deep symbolic meaning. My gift is a lot uglier than that, but it has deep meaning for me.

"I have been so mad for so long at so many things, especially at You and me. Until now, I had forgotten how beautiful You are and how ugly I have made you. I am so sorry."

Again, Tyler had to pause to react emotionally. He wasn't used to talking to his Savior in this way. He wasn't used to talking with Him at all.

"So I'm bringing you all my hurt and all my bitterness. That's my gift to You. I don't know what else to do with it. All I know is that I can't carry it around anymore. I know I have a lot to learn about You, and I have a lot to work through, but I'm handing this over right now.

"Help me to always see You as I do right now. Help me not to forget Your beautiful face and penetrating eyes. Help me to destroy the old canvas of You I had constructed and start anew. I don't want to blame You anymore."

That was all he could say. He hoped it was enough. Tyler sat in reverent silence for minutes with intermittent tears emerging to provide a healing balm over the spiritual sores that had festered for so many years. He looked upon the entire scene with a full heart and great appreciation. Only now did he understand his mother's devotion. He vowed to follow her example, as he quieted himself at this makeshift tabernacle.

Tyler, I am proud of you.

The thought was foreign to him yet unavoidable. He almost looked around to see where it came from. He even looked at the baby in the manger to see if he would offer a deferential wink. Then he realized it came from within. Was it wishful thinking? He wasn't used to pondering such things. Maybe he was trying to make himself feel better. Or, more likely, he reasoned, his mind was finally uncluttered of its usual doubt and skepticism, and he was finally hearing the truth. He decided to take it on faith and receive what the Lord freely offered.

He remained there for at least half an hour, reflecting on the day's events and becoming more keenly aware of His orchestration of them. He also had an unshakable sense that the Lord's presence wasn't limited to this roadside display but would continue with him now and forever.

"Young man, could you tell me what you're doing over there?"

The question jolted Tyler from his spiritual summit meeting. Still seated on the ground, he turned and looked over his shoulder to see a police car parked with the engine running and an officer in the passenger's seat yelling through his open window.

"I said, what are you doing over there?"

Quickly rising to his feet and turning toward the officer, he instinctively put both hands in the air and said, "Oh nothing. Just praying, I guess."

"Praying? You know there are a lot better places to pray tonight, right?"

Approaching the police car, Tyler said, "Yeah. I understand. This one just seemed to work best for me."

"And how much have you had to drink tonight?" the officer inquired.

"Not enough," Tyler jokingly replied, now mere feet from the patrolman's car window. Realizing this wasn't the ideal time for humor, he said, "I haven't had any alcohol, sir. I don't drink."

Being close enough to smell his breath and size him up, and seeing that he had no difficulty in walking, the officer seemed to believe him. "Where's home for you?"

"Uh, it's just a few blocks from here. My car is actually parked on East 40th. I'm headed back to it now."

"I think that's a good idea," the officer said authoritatively. "You need a ride?"

"No, I should be all right," Tyler responded.

"All right then. Merry Christmas."

"Merry Christmas," Tyler returned. As the car pulled away and Tyler began walking toward his car, he realized he had worn a broad smile on his face throughout his conversation. No wonder they were tempted to do a sobriety test. He couldn't stop laughing to himself the entire walk back to his car. He couldn't remember the last time he had been mistaken for a happy person. He knew the look suited him.

Retrieving his car and driving the final few blocks to his apartment, he knew that he should collapse into his bed to ponder everything he had encountered. However, sleep was the farthest thing from his mind. His heart was so full that he knew he needed to do something in response. Sure, the time would come when he could finally rest in gratitude for what he had experienced.

But there was one thing left to be done.

Thirteen

Wally and Jackie Bennett were early risers. They couldn't remember at what point it occurred. They each had their own theory as to why they remained so in their later years. Jackie always blamed it on having to be at work at 7 a.m. for so many years, saying her body clock had permanently adjusted to it. Wally had a completely different take on it, which he loved to share with anyone who would give him a few minutes to explain. "You see," Wally would pontificate, "I have one reason for getting out of bed when I do each morning: pain." He would follow it up with his usual expulsion of humorous air and continue. "When you get to be my age, you stay in bed until it just hurts to remain there, which for me is about 5 o'clock." If Jackie was nearby, she would invariably shake her head in playful embarrassment.

Tyler was counting on their love of routine this Christmas morning. Wally would be the first to be roused from slumber. He had long mastered the art of extricating himself from the bed without waking his beloved. About the only sound he would make would be an occasional grunt as he put his weight on his feet to stand on the carpeted floor. From there, he would splash some water on his face and brush his teeth before walking into the living room. His routine on Saturdays and holidays was predictable. He loved making breakfast for Jackie and having it ready for her shortly after she emerged to face the day. However, she would often remain asleep for an undetermined period of time, so Wally would make a pot of coffee and set out what he needed until he heard Jackie stirring.

While the coffee would slowly dispense into the carafe, Wally would retrieve his morning paper from the front porch, sit in his comfortable chair, and read it until his spouse awakened. His local paper printed editions even on major holidays, so he could start Christmas morning with his usual pattern.

On a still-dark December 25th morning, wearing pajamas and slippers, Wally arose, entered the kitchen, and made a half-pot of regular coffee, or "diesel" as he liked to call it. It was his one vice, Jackie liked to point out. He would drink a couple of cups before leaving for work and continue consuming at regular intervals into the afternoon at his business. Frequently toting his, "I Love My Boss" mug around the office, he often told clients that he liked to drink coffee the way people vote in Chicago: early and often. His other favorite coffee joke was saved for church folk; more specifically, newer members of the congregation who had not yet heard his material. "You know coffee is in the Bible don't ya?" he would ask an unwitting straight-man in the church lobby. "Oh yeah. In fact, it's so important that a whole book of the Bible is named for it: He Brews." Never to be mistaken for a professional comedian, his stabs at humor were just folksy enough to win anyone over.

As the coffee slowly dripped through the filter and into the pot, he headed toward the front door to retrieve the newspaper and see what shape the world was in this Christmas morn. The Bennetts had planned to have Tyler over in the afternoon for gifts and eventually dinner. Jackie would prepare her famed lasagna and garlic bread with cheese. Wally's scrambled eggs and bacon would more than satisfy their appetite until then.

Opening the wooden front door, he was surprised to see a carefully wrapped bundle next to his newspaper. Suddenly forgetting his purpose for going outside, he picked up the gift-wrapped stack. It had been tied together in red ribbon with a large bow on top. The gift on the bottom was thin and rectangular. Its neighbor above was smaller in overall size but thicker. At its apex was an envelope with the words, "Open First" decoratively written on it. The unexpected display of kindness was too much for Wally to contain. "Ma! Wake up! We've got us a Christmas surprise."

"Hmmm, what is it?" Jackie uttered in a muffled tone from the bedroom.

"Someone left us some gifts on our doorstep, Ma! You gotta see this!"

"All right," she said kindly but groggy. "I'll be there in a minute."

Wearing her colorful Christmas pajamas and robe, she stepped into the living room, her hair unkempt and eyes halfway open, to see the package specially delivered to their porch.

"I do believe Santa stopped by last night," Wally offered, the more jovial of the two in the morning and the more childlike in general.

"All right now," Jackie said, almost in a motherly fashion. "Who's it from?"

"I don't know. I haven't opened it yet."

Jackie surveyed the contents. "What do you think they might be?"

"You got me," Wally said. "All I know is that I didn't hear any ticking inside the boxes, which is always a good sign."

Jackie privately enjoyed the way her husband turned into an eight-year-old at moments like this. "Well, I guess we should follow orders and open the envelope first."

"All right. You do the honors."

Jackie grabbed her reading glasses from the table next to her recliner and put them on the bridge of her nose. Holding the bow with one hand, she slid the envelope out with the other and examined it, carefully studying the calligraphy. "I have a feeling I know who this is from."

"Yeah. Me too," Wally said.

Using her thumbnail, she slid open the envelope much more elegantly than Wally, who would have annihilated it in anticipation of reading its contents. Jackie began reading aloud:

"Dear Mr. and Mrs. B: I haven't slept since you last saw me after the church service. Don't worry. I'm OK. More than OK, actually.

"I want to apologize for doing this with such short notice, but I won't be able to join you later for dinner. I love you both very much, but I can't remember a time in my life when I have been more inspired. To try to explain the last 24 hours would be almost impossible. I will tell you about it soon, but it will be hard to understand, even for you. All I know is that I can't waste a moment with how I feel right now. Sorry. It's the perils of being friends with an artist.

"I wanted to express my love and thanks to you for being the wonderful people you are. Please accept these gifts as the absolute best way of conveying my deepest thoughts and feelings for you. Mr. B, yours is on the bottom. Miss-, I mean, Jackie (See, I remembered!), yours is on top. Please read the inside cover. There's an inscription I wrote a year ago, but it applies today just as much if not more.

"Thanks for being Dad and Mom to a struggling artist and a struggling man trying to figure things out. I love you. Tyler."

Neither Wally nor Jackie moved or even spoke for a few minutes. Jackie removed her glasses, placed them back on the end table, folded the note, and returned it into the envelope. Eventually, Jackie wiped back a few tears and Wally placed his arm around her, massaging her shoulder.

"Well, you ready for the moment of truth?" Wally asked.

Jackie politely nodded her assent. Wally carefully removed the bow and untied the ribbon, allowing it to fall at either side of the stack. He handed the top present to his wife, who placed it on her lap. By her expression and stillness, she wanted Wally to open his first.

Wally was only happy to oblige. Holding it with both hands, he could tell that one side of the gift gave way, that the wrapping paper was not flush against a surface. "I wonder what it could be," he wondered.

Jackie, usually quicker on the trigger, said, "I have a guess," but added nothing more.

Tearing the paper at what he believed was the backside of the gift, he realized he was right. It was the back of a wooden frame. Removing all the paper and flipping it over, Wally realized he was holding Tyler's latest creation in his hands. Measuring three feet across and two feet high, it was the completion of a beautiful Christmas scene that had looked so chaotic in Tyler's loft the previous day. The tree had been painted with exquisite precision. He had never seen so many shades of green all blended together so masterfully. The lights, tinsel, and ornaments all demanded great attention to the viewer, but what arrested the eye was the bright white star on top. It was a lot to take in.

"Ma, this is the most beautiful thing he has ever painted," Wally said in wonder. "Isn't it something?"

Jackie, overwhelmed by its beauty, placed both hands over her mouth in excitement over what had been given and the extent to which Tyler's talent had improved. Wally brought the painting closer to his wife, kneeling next to Jackie's chair, so they could both admire it. They spent the next half hour taking in every hue and brushstroke, examining individual ornaments on the branches and multi-colored lights all screaming for attention.

Wally finally broke the awesome silence. "I know I leave all the decorating stuff to you, but I want this picture to hang in our house all year long, I don't care if it is a Christmas painting. This needs to be seen as often as possible."

Patting his shoulder, Jackie said, "I agree, honey, and I know just the place for it." Wally wouldn't make any more demands. He would delegate the rest of the task to his wife. He just wanted to make sure it wouldn't be left in the attic for ten months of the year. Just then, Jackie had a sudden burst of remembrance. "Oh, sweetie! Can you read the title of the painting? I took off my glasses."

Wally, with not much better vision than his wife and not wanting to go through the effort of putting in his contact lenses, grasped the painting with both hands and held it only inches from his face. As usual, Tyler had blended the title into the color scheme of the painting. "It's really small this time...let me see if I've got it here...it says, "Every...Ornament...Has..." Wally's voice trailed off and he lifted his gaze from the canvas and chuckled. "Well, I'll be!"

"What? Every ornament has what?" Jackie wondered.

"It's something I said to Tyler yesterday that my mother always said. 'Every ornament has a story.'" Wally looked off into the distance with overwhelming sentimentality. The gift itself had been deeply personal, but the thought behind it filled his heart with love and gratitude. "I don't even know what to say."

Jackie added, "Now that's a Christmas miracle!"

Both of them shared a laugh as Wally stood and leaned the gift against a nearby wall. "All right, Ma, let's see what you got."

Jackie took the gift from its resting place on her lap and carefully removed the wrapping paper with much greater precision than her husband, tearing along natural creases in the paper. Wally had long learned not to interrupt this procedure. In their earlier married years, their methods of opening gifts frequently caused quarrels, Jackie believing her husband tore into gifts like a tiger into a dying wildebeest, and Wally bemoaned her methods, thinking every gift was the equivalent of the Hope Diamond. While some older couples made such things a source of common bickering in their later years, they had long ago called a truce to such trivial skirmishes.

Though it never happened, theoretically the paper used for one of Jackie's gifts was removed with such care that it could undoubtedly be used again. As she dislodged the clear tape from the gift and unfolded the wrapping paper, she removed the small white box inside. Lifting its tight lid, she quickly realized what she had received. It was the back of a brown leather Bible. Opening it up, she immediately started flipping pages until she stopped somewhere in the Psalms. "Oh sweetie! It's a parallel Bible."

"Hey, that's all right!" Wally announced. "Maybe you can use that for your morning devotions."

"Definitely," Jackie said. She decided to try it out by reading aloud one of her favorite scripture passages, Psalm 91. Retrieving her glasses, she read through it in the traditional King James. Wally could have quoted it with her, but he sat quietly and allowed her to have full command of the moment. She then read it in the parallel version to its side, with Wally listening intently. When she finished, Jackie said, "That is so thoughtful of him," and closed the Bible. That was when she first saw a name engraved on the front cover: "ELIZABETH RAMSEY".

Jackie gasped at the discovery. Her husband was startled by her sudden reaction. "Oh Wally! This was his mother's Bible."

"Are you serious?" Wally stood and walked behind Jackie's chair and beheld the Bible over his wife's shoulder. To them, it was like discovering a valuable antique at a flea market. "Tyler said there was an inscription on the inside."

Deliberately, Jackie turned over the leather cover. With the same style of calligraphy used on the envelope, she read an old but meaningful message, "*To the greatest woman I know*."

Jackie removed her glasses and began tearing up. Wally leaned over and placed one arm around her, occasionally turning his head so he could kiss her on the cheek. There he remained until his wife had expressed all that needed to be expressed.

Hardly a word was spoken in the Bennett house that morning. After what they had unwrapped, mere words would only taint the purity of the joy they felt. The air was too rich, too sublime to be marred by human observations or platitudes. They felt only a deeper satisfaction for the young man they had believed in for so long who now finally believed in himself.

Tyler actually did sleep for a few hours that morning, but he was too anxious to remain there long. Before surrendering to fatigue a few hours earlier, he had already set up his new project. It would be larger in scale than his previous works, two-feet across and five-feet tall. Hoping not to forget the subject, he had taken the liberty of titling the work along the bottom edge.

By 8 o'clock Christmas morning, he sprang out of bed, put on a comfortable T-shirt and sweat pants, and started some coffee. He turned on the TV near the Christmas tree he had so carefully assembled and painted. It was designed to provide some white noise and ease him into his creative mode while he drank his coffee. It was one of the national early-morning talk shows, with substitute hosts in place of the show's usual pairing.

Still a bit haggard from the previous night's adventures, Tyler reclined on the sofa and looked about the loft at the Christmas tree that had been constructed, the bins he had retrieved a little more than 24 hours ago, and finally at his studio. He pondered all that he had seen and experienced and was overwhelmed. As the TV show recited news headlines and the national weather forecast, Tyler closed his eyes and thought about what had changed in his heart.

In that moment, he came to a stirring spiritual conclusion. Though he had been a Christian since childhood, last night was the first time he could call himself a believer. Life and experience had eroded his faith in so many areas. Now he was a believer again. These things weren't just true in a general sense; they now applied to him. He could not remember the last time he had started a day believing that God was for him, but he knew it now. That's why he was out of bed with only a couple of hours of sleep. He had to capitalize on this moment.

He rose from the sofa and turned off the television, disinterested in global affairs and weather fronts. With coffee cup in hand, he turned on Christmas music, playing it with a higher volume than usual, knowing he had the entire building to himself. It filled the loft like a department store full of last-minute shoppers. From there, he walked to his studio and placed his cup on the small table to his left. He looked at the blank space before him, but he wasn't intimidated by it. He already had a clear vision of his finished work and looked forward to his first flourish.

Looking again at the bottom of the canvas, he saw what he had titled the new work the night before. What in the world made him think he would forget it? He just wanted to make sure, realizing how fleeting creative waves can be. As he built the backdrop of the painting, he would add shadings and subtle additions to the black letters now present: REAL JESUS. He didn't know what he would do with it when it was finished, and he frankly didn't care. He was only thankful to have awakened today with a greater sense of purpose than he had known in his entire life. Figuratively, Tyler Ramsey had come in from the outside.

He started painting.

Made in the USA
Lexington, KY
06 November 2017